D1596984

Telegrams of the Soul

Selected Prose of Peter Altenberg

Selected, translated and
with an afterword by Peter Wortsman

a r c h i p e l a g o   b o o k s

Library of Congress Cataloging-in-Publication Data
Altenberg, Peter, 1859–1919.
[Prose works. Selections. English. 2005]
Telegrams of the soul : selected prose of Peter Altenberg /
selected, translated, and with an afterword by Peter Wortsman.
— 1st ed.
p. cm.
ISBN 0-9749680-8-0 (pbk.)
1. Altenberg, Peter, 1859-1919 — Translations into English.
I. Wortsman, Peter. II. Title.
PT2601.L78A6 2005
838'.91208 — dc22   2004027895

Archipelago Books
25 Jay Street #203
Brooklyn, NY 11201
www.archipelagobooks.org

Distributed by Consortium Book Sales and Distribution
1045 Westgate Dr.
St. Paul, MN 55114
www.cbsd.com

Telegrams of the Soul: Selected Prose of Peter Altenberg

Translations of "Flower Allée," "The Mouse" and "In the
Stadtpark" were first published in *Fiction*. An earlier
version of "P.S. (to P.A. from P.W.)" previously appeared under
a different title in *A Modern Way to Die, small stories and microtales*,
by Peter Wortsman, Fromm International Publishing Corporation,
New York, 1991.

This publication is made possible with public funds from the
New York State Council on the Arts, a state agency.

NYSCA

to my father's wit and my mother's soul

P. W.

Contents

There are three idealists: God, mothers and poets!
They don't seek the ideal in completed things —
they find it in the incomplete.

Peter Altenberg

Telegrams of the Soul

Autobiography

I was born in 1862, in Vienna. My father is a businessman. He has one distinguishing quality: He only reads French books. For the past 40 years. Above his bed hangs a wonderful likeness of his God "Victor Hugo." Evenings he sits in a dark red armchair, reading the *Revue des deux Mondes*, dressed in a blue robe with a wide velvet collar à la Victor Hugo. There's not another idealist like him in this world. He was once asked: "Aren't you proud of your son?"

He replied: "I was not overly vexed that he remained an idler for 30 years. So I'm not overly honored that he's a poet now! I gave him his freedom. I knew that it was a long shot. I counted on his soul!"

Yes, indeed, oh noblest, most remarkable of all fathers, for the longest time I squandered your godly gift of freedom, doted on noble and altogether ignoble women, loafed around in forests, was a lawyer without studying law, a doctor without studying medicine, a book dealer without selling books, a lover without ever marrying, and finally a poet without composing any poetry. Can these short things really be called poetry?! No way. They're extracts! Extracts from life. The life of the soul and what the day may bring, reduced to two to three pages, cleansed of superfluities like a beef cow in a reduction pot! It's up to the reader to re-dissolve these extracts with his own lust for life and stir them back into a palatable broth, to heat them up with his own zest, in short, to make them light, liquidy and digestible. But there are "soulful stomachs" that can't tolerate extracts. Everything ingested remains heavy and caustic. Such constitutions require 90 percent broths, watered-down blends. What are they supposed to dilute the extracts with?! With their own "lust for life" maybe?

Consequently, I have many adversaries, "dyspeptics of the soul," quite simply. Bad digesters! "Finishing" is the artist's all. Even finishing with himself! And yet, I maintain: that which you "wisely withhold" is more artistic than that which you "blurt out." Isn't that so?! Indeed, I love the "abbreviated deal," the telegram style of the soul!

I'd like to capture an individual in a single sentence, a soul-stirring experience on a single page, a landscape in one word! Present arms, artist, aim, bull's-eye! Basta. And above all: Listen to yourself. Lend an ear to the voices within. Don't be shy with yourself. Don't let yourself be scared off by unfamiliar sounds. As long as they're your own! Have the courage of your own nakedness!

I was nothing, I am nothing, I will be nothing. But I will live out my life in freedom and let noble and considerate souls share in the experiences of this free inner life, by putting them out in the most concentrated form on paper.

I am poor, but I am myself! Absolutely and completely myself! The man without compromises!

How far do you get with that? One hundred Guldens a month and a few ardent admirers.

Well, that's what I've got.

My life has been devoted to the boundless admiration of God's artwork, "woman's body!" The walls of my humble room are practically papered over with perfect studies of the nude. All are hung in oaken frames with captions. A fifteen-year-old bears the motto: "Beauté est vertue." Beneath another it says: "There is but one indecency in the naked — to deem the naked indecent!"

Under yet another it says: "This is how God and the poets dreamed you up. But feeble little man invented modesty and covered you, en-coffined you!"

When P.A. wakes, his glance falls on the holy splendor and he takes the trouble and stress of existence in stride, since he was endowed with two eyes to drink in the holiest loveliness on earth!

Eye, oh eye, Rothchild-chattel of man!

But the others stare, they ogle life like the toad ogles the water-lily.

I'd like these words inscribed on my tombstone: "He loved and saw."

Yes, indeed, to live in inner ecstasies, to get yourself all hot and bothered, piping hot, to let yourself be set on fire by the beauties of this world, that was all we ever wanted, father and son, that was all.

But whereas the old man was still somewhat attached to everyday life, at times colliding with it, the younger one fled immediately and without a second thought from this dungeon of duty.

True, I am poor, poor, but my noble father gave me the treasure which few fathers in their gentle wisdom grant their sons: "Time for development and freedom." That allowed my uncorrupted soul to lovingly abandon itself to the inconceivable treasures which every hour of every day spill like pearls onto the desolate shore of life, allowed it to abandon itself to the tragic or the tender events, and grow, grow —.

My Mama was once a very delicate, strikingly lovely lady with fine hands and feet and slender joints. Like a gazelle. Once my father brought back from England a very pretty girl. He said to Mama: "This, my dear, is Maud-Victoria. She is the prettiest girl in England." My Mama saw that she was indeed the prettiest girl in England and said in a downright sorrowful voice: "Will she have to stay with us from now on?" Whereupon, my father was so moved that he sent the "prettiest girl in England" back where she came from.

When my father paid frequent visits to the Ashantee girls,* my dearly beloved girlfriends, and gave them silk scarves as gifts, everyone said: "The old man and his son are two of a kind."

As a boy I had an indescribable love for mountain meadows. The mountain meadow steaming under the blazing sun, fragrantly wafting, alive with bugs and butterflies, made me downright drunk. So too did clearings in the woods. On swampy sunny patches sit butterflies, blue silken small ones and black and red admirals and you can see the hoofprint of deer. But for mountain meadows I had a fanatical love, I longed for them. Under all the white hot stones I imagined there lurked poison adders, and this creature was the very incarnation of the fairy tale mystery of my boyhood years. It replaced the man-eating ogre, the giant and the witch. All the bites and their consequences, the terribly slow and torturous pain, I knew it all by heart, how to treat a wound and so

---

*In 1897, Altenberg often visited, promptly befriended and idolized the subjects, especially the young women, of a live human exhibit of Africans from the Gold Coast in a reconstructed village erected at Vienna's Zoological Garden in the Schönbrunn Palace Gardens. A curious example of Fin-de-Siècle flirtation with the exotic, Altenberg, characteristically, metamorphosed that flirtation into a heartfelt passion.

on. The wondrously delicate gray-black body of the adder seemed to me to be the loveliest, most elegant creature, and when I loved a little girl I always pictured again and again only one thing happening: an adder would bite her in the foot on a hike and I'd suck out the venom to save her!

I knew the terrain inside out in which adders must necessarily make their homes, trod through it, lay in wait; but in my entire life I have never spotted a live adder, even though the region around Schneeberg is crawling with them. It remained for me a bad but sweetly disturbing dream.

Ever and again I imagined the scene: my beloved is bitten, above the ankle. Everyone stands around helpless and desperate. Then I fetch a flask of gentian root spirit from the nearest chalet, engender the proper state of intoxication, the only remedy. Then she says: "Heavens, however did you know that?" And I say simply: "I read it in Brehm—"

Always, everywhere I waited for adders. They never came.

At age 23, I worshiped a thirteen-year-old girl, wept through my nights, got engaged to her, became a book dealer in Stuttgart so as to hurry up and earn enough money to be able to fend for her later. But nothing came of it. Nothing ever came of my dreams.

I never found anything else in life worthwhile except for a woman's beauty, the grace of a lady, so sweet, so childlike! And I view anyone who ever prized anything else as a poor fool swindled out of his life!

Give your all to the implacable day and the merciless hour, but know it and feel it that your holiest and truest moments are only those in which your stirred and stunned eye falls upon a female graceful and soft! Better know it, life's lackey, that you're a day laborer, a carter, a prisoner, a recruit, a self-deceiver deceived by life, and that only by the grace of a "saintly lovely woman" could you ever rise to an aristocrat or king!

I only value the little things I write insofar as they shed a little light for the man drawn and drained by a thousand duties on the lovely, graceful and mysterious being at his side. Consumed by the tasks of his implacable day, he dare not view woman as a rare and inscrutable being in and of herself, but rather as nothing more than a partner in his miseries! Her world is dear and understandable to him only insofar as he derives blessings from it. The other life is left to the poets! Thus do these souls ever so slightly removed from life take up their lyres again and again to exalt with their tears the noble creatures of which the others take brutal advantage! I myself have only suffered at the foot of these beauties to whom I have consecrated my lost and unnecessary existence. Still I believe I had a hand in infusing a whiff of the Greek cult of beauty in the harried life of a few young fools! But that too may only be a utopia.

Poor and forsaken, I live out what's left of my life, my glance still seeking out a noble woman's hand, a graceful step, a gentle face turned away from the world. Amen—.

Retrospective Introduction to my Book
Märchen des Lebens *

We relegated fairytales to the realm of childhood—that exceptional, wondrous, stirring, remarkable time of life! But why rig out childhood with it, when childhood is already sufficiently romantic and fairytale-like in and of itself? The disenchanted adult had best seek out the fairytale-like elements, the romanticism of each day and each hour right here and now in the hard, stern, cold fundament of life! Even the truly predestined poets with their more impressionable hearts, eyes and ears fetch their telling tidbits from actual occurrences, listening in on the romance of life itself. The rest of us can all become poets too if only we take pains not to let slip a single pearl which life in its rich bounty tosses up every now and then onto the flat dreary beachhead of our day!

Everything is remarkable if our perception of it is remarkable! And every little local incident written up in the daily newspaper can sound the depths of life, revealing all the tragic and the comic, the same as Shakespeare's tragedies! We all do life an injustice in surrendering poetry as the exclusive province of the poet's heart, since every one of us has the capacity to mine the poetic in the quarry of the mundane! The poet's heart will forfeit this privilege through the evolution of the intrinsic culture of the common human heart!

---

* *Märchen des Lebens* (The Fairytale of Life), 1908

A Letter to Arthur Schnitzler

July 1894

Dear Dr. Arthur Schnitzler,

Your lovely letter made me truly inordinately happy. So how do I write?

Altogether freely, without any deliberation. I never know my subject beforehand, I never think it over. I just take paper and write. Even the title I toss off and hope that what comes out will have something to do with it.

One must have confidence, not force the issue, just let oneself live life to the fullest, frightfully free, let it fly — .

What comes out is definitely the stuff that was real and deep down in me. If nothing comes out then there was nothing real and deep down in me and that doesn't matter then either.

I view writing as a natural organic spilling out of a full, overripe person. Thus the failings, the pale cast of thought.

I hate any revision. Toss it off and that's good — ! Or bad! What's the difference?! If it's only you, you and nobody else, your sacred you. The term you coined "self-searcher" is really terrific. But when will you write "self-finder"?

My pieces have the misfortune always to be taken for little rehearsals, whereas they are, alas, already the very best I can do. But what's the difference?! I couldn't care less if I write or not.

The more important thing is that I be able to show in a circle of refined, cultured young people that the little spark is fluttering in me. Otherwise, one has the impression of seeming so pressed, so importunate, as if everyone looked askance. I'm already enough of an "invalid of life." Your letter made me very very happy! You're all so kind to me. Everyone full of goodwill. But you really did say such absolutely wonderful things to me. Especially that term "self-searcher."

With no profession, no money, no position and already hardly any hair, you can well imagine that such gracious recognition from a "man in the know" falls on very welcome ears.

Thus am I and will I ever remain a writer of "worthless samples" and the finished product never appears. I'm just a kind of little pocket mirror, powder mirror, no world-mirror.

Yours,
Peter Altenberg

On Writing

I just came to the realization, to the sudden, illuminating, simple realization, upon receipt of a letter from my true friend, Fr. W., a man most inclined to friendship (he writes with unbelievable verve on one of the finest typewriters) that to write a good letter can only mean to write it such that the recipient be able, while reading it, to hear the letter writer speaking loudly and most emphatically to him, as though seated right there at his side! To be able to completely reconcile in a letter this difference between the one who silently writes and the one who speaks out loud, that's true letter writing skill! Everything else is literary rubbish crowned with laurels à la pig's head. Temperament, incivilities, peculiarities, impertinences, tomfooleries, everything must come roaring out, roaring, roaring; or else it's a contrived, mendacious and, therefore, boring, business! Letter-instant-photography!

A friend of mine, the watchmaker Josef T., once came to me with a request. He had just laid his lovely 23-year-old beloved in the grave.

"Peter, you know me, please help me! Write me a proper inscription for my marble tombstone. When may I hope that you think up something appropriate?"

"Now or never!" I replied right there in the middle of the street.

He tore out his notebook.

I wrote:

"I was the Watchmaker Josef T.,
And then I found paradise through you —.
And now I'm the Watchmaker
Joseph T. again —."

You've got to pour out all your humanity spontaneously, in a rush; because later it turns into a tasteless sauce! That's why there are so many tasteless sauces —.

The *Koberer* (Procurer)

"Own up," said the Count to Mitzi G., "who'd you get to draft this letter to me for you?!"

"Drafted?! Drafted?! What do you mean by that?!"

"Drafted! You couldn't possibly have dreamed it up yourself!"

"Why not?! You think I'm all that stupid?!"

"No, yes. But once and for all, you didn't write this letter!"

"Who else do you think wrote it?!"

"That I don't know. You're the only one that knows it. Listen, Mitzi, I'll give you one hundred Crowns if you tell his name!"

"One hundred Crowns? Make it one fifty!"

"It was Peter!"

"What Peter?!"

"Peter, you know, Peter Altenberg!"

The letter: "Saw you again last night at the 'Tabarin!' Couldn't talk to you, didn't dare to. So there I was seated face to face with the guy that had me for a whole year butt-naked under the covers. . . . It was just no use!"

"How did he ever come to draft this letter for you?!"

I said to him, I said: "For God's sake, write me something I'd have written if I knew how to write!"

"So the letter's from you after all?!"

"That's what I said from the start!"

So then she patched things up again with the Count.

Coffeehouse

You've got troubles of one kind or another — get thee to the coffee-house!

She can't make it to your place for whatever perfectly plausible reason — to the coffeehouse!

Your boots are torn — to the coffeehouse!

You make four hundred Crowns and spend five hundred — coffeehouse!

You're a frugal fellow and don't dare spend a penny on yourself — coffeehouse!

You're a paper pusher and would've liked to become a doctor — coffeehouse!

You can't find a girlfriend up to snuff — coffeehouse!

You're virtually on the verge of suicide — coffeehouse!

You loathe and revile people and yet can't live without them — coffeehouse!

No place else will let you pay on credit — coffeehouse!

I Drink Tea

Six P.M. approaches. I sense it coming on. Not as intensely as the children sense the approach of Christmas Eve. But I sense it all the same. At six on the dot I drink tea, a festive satisfaction that never disappoints in this burdensome existence. Something you can count on, to have a becalming bliss at your beck and call. A given completely free of life's vicissitudes. Pouring the good mountain spring water into my lovely white half-liter nickel-plated receptacle already gives me pleasure. Then I wait out the simmer, the song of the water. I have a huge, semispherical, deep, brick-red Wedgewood cup. The tea comes from the Café Central, wafting with the scent of high mountain meadow, of wild bugle and sunburned pasture grass.

The tea is golden yellow-straw yellow, never brownish, always light and unoppressive. I smoke a cigarette along with it, a "Chelmis, Hyksos." I sip it very very slowly. The tea is an internally stimulating nerve bath. You can bear it all better while drinking it. You feel it inside, a woman ought to have that effect. But she never does. She hasn't yet acquired the culture of serene sweetness so as to affect you like a noble warm golden-yellow tea. She believes she'd lose her power. But my six o'clock tea never loses its power over me. I long for it daily in just the same way and lovingly let it wed my body.

Perfume

As a child, rummaging around a drawer in the desk of my beloved, oh so beautiful Mama, the desk made of mahogany and cut glass, I found an empty perfume bottle which still retained the potent scent of a certain unidentified fragrance.

Many times I'd sneak over and sniff at it.

I associated this fragrance with all the love, tenderness, friendship, longing, sadness in the world. But for me all these feelings were bound up with my Mama. Later fate fell upon us, unsuspected, like a horde of Huns and inflicted heavy losses all around.

And one day I dashed from perfumery to perfumery hoping to possibly find in the little sample bottles the fragrance from the mahogany desk drawer of my late beloved Mama. And finally, finally I found it: Peau d'Espagne, Pinaud, from Paris.

And I remembered the bygone days when Mama was the only womanly presence able to arouse pleasure and pain, ardent longing and deep despair, but who would always, always forgive whatever I'd done and who fretted over me and perhaps even before falling asleep at night prayed for my future happiness . . .

Later, many young women in their guileless sweet zeal sent me their favorite perfume to thank me from the heart for a beauty tip of my devising, namely that every perfume ought to be rubbed into the skin all over the naked body right after the bath so that it wafts forth like the body's own true natural essence! But all these perfumes were like the scents of breathtakingly beautiful but rather poisonous exotic flowers. Only the fragrance Peau d'Espagne, Pinaud, from Paris, brought me a melancholic tranquility, even though Mama was no longer there and could no longer forgive me for my sins!

On Smells

Women are enormously impressionable, they so easily take on the smells of their surroundings! If she was in the dairy, then for hours afterwards she'll smell of milk, her hands, her hair, her entire body—. If she was at the green grocers, she'll retain for hours the smell of all the greens, like a mixed vegetable soup—. In the garden she smells of lilacs or linden trees or just of garden—. On the high mountain meadow of cow pasture land and fresh cut meadow. This is a tragic fate; since she always smells afterwards of the last lout she was with, of the last snob and his repulsive scent, his foul odor of duplicity! She never smells of poets since poets keep a respectful distance, probably on account of their artistic egotism. Most often women smell of "smart alecks" always too close for comfort! That's when they are most receptive to smells—. Noble ladies definitely ought to remain outdoors in nature or stick to the saintly solitude of their own domicile. It stinks everywhere else!

Even good books never stink, they are the distillation of all the malodorous sins one has committed of which one has finally managed to extract a drop of fragrant humanity!

But the other sins can't be distilled!

Tulips

There are geniuses among the tulips, too, just as there are in every manifestation of the organic! Like orchids, for instance. I once had a white tulip that stayed shut tight, immaculate and virginal, for a full fourteen days despite the warmth of my room and water. Only then did it open and brazenly display its stamen and its pistil. And so it remained for another eight days. Others, for instance, will open on the spot in a warm room and water, and are already complete in all their splendor; their petals fall as if stunned by the blow. Still others, especially the speckled ones, evidently just shrivel up like little old grannies, without losing their petals they die off, doggedly resisting life. You throw them away even though there could still be a little spare life left in them! And it may well be so. Tulips are not without smell, they exude to the eyes! It may well be the most exciting, longest lasting scent there is!

Flower Allée

Six A.M. It is dry, cool, the sky is a wan white blue, *bleu-lacté* the French writers would say—.

A florist dealing in artificial flowers flings back gray wooden shutters, open for business.

In the dusty window display, spring blooms in sloe blossoms; summer in cornflowers; fall in pink and lilac asters and the feathery pompoms of dandelions.

A pale shop girl carries white roses out into the street, with which she decorates a carriage parked outside. The flowers smell like old muslin.

Flower Allée—or this afternoon at four! Box seats, five crowns! Let 'em spread the money among the people, thousands profit indirectly, you have no idea! It trickles down to—Why it's just impossible to think it all the way through.

Out in the street, a young woman with a sleeping child in her arms stares at the "flying bed of roses," a slice of "enchantment," roses and a horse-drawn carriage, the mystery of the "beautiful superfluous!"

The child sleeps soundly in the clear morning air.

From a first floor window, a young prostitute in her nightgown peeks out from behind a white shade: "Should I hire the carriage, should I not, should I, should I not, should I—?"

The shop girl looks up: "Slut—!"

The shop girl yawns, sticks a rose into the coachman's buttonhole.

The young mother with the child walks on. The child sleeps soundly in the clear morning air.

The prostitute pulls down the shade.

The rose-carriage rolls off; the roses sway, bow, rustle, tremble in the breeze, and one tumbles to the asphalt—

That afternoon, a woman and a young girl hire the carriage.

"Les fleurs sont fausses—," the girl observes.

"'S 'at so—," says the woman, "is it really that obvious?!"

Flower Allée. Access via the Praterstrasse. Flying flower bed. Thousands profit indirectly!

The young prostitute lies in her bed, asleep. The afternoon sun warms the white shade. She is dreaming: "Rose carriage —."

The shop girl reclines on a little whicker chair in the dark, dank artificial flower storeroom, asleep —. She is dreaming: "Rose carriage —."

The young woman carries her child through the streets. The child sleeps soundly in the misty afternoon air —.

The rose that tumbled that morning from the passing carriage stands tall in a glass on a street sweeper's window sill.

His little daughter says: "Yuck, it stinks —."

To which the street sweeper might have replied: "These are the flowers that blossom on the asphalt of a big city —!" But that's not what he said. A simple man — it just wasn't his way —. He muses: "Must be from the Flower Allée —!"

Uncle Max

This Max, my uncle, who's been dead for seven years now, was once very handsome, indeed, extremely handsome, even according to modern standards. Exceedingly slender, exceedingly tall, and with a pug nose. Consequently, he had a love affair with his mother's, my grand-mamma's, very young seamstress. He bought himself a small villa with garden in Hietzing, on the High Street, and installed his seamstress there. She planted herself a bed of roses and carnations and was pleased that her dainty lovely little fingers no longer had to suffer from all the sewing. She even nursed them now with malatine and honey glycerin to make up for those awful torturous years. One day the family decided that my tall, handsome, slender uncle with the pug nose ought to make a "match." "Alright," he said, "à la bonheur. But what will become of Anna?" Anna was married off to a man who had been terribly fond of her since childhood and had only lacked "nervus rerum" to make her — pardon, himself, happy! Anna went along with everything, since it is better to go along with things when not to go along with them is of little use. So my uncle married and added another floor to the villa in Hietzing. A gardener was engaged to tend to the rose and carnation beds planted by Anna. One day my newlywed aunt said to my tall, handsome, slender uncle: "Say, who was that Anna anyway after whom these lovely well-kept carnations are named?" My uncle peered down at the speckled carnations and could not fathom why this Anna still mattered.

My uncle has been dead and gone for seven years now and my aunt is a grand-mamma. The only thing that hasn't changed is the lovely bed of speckled Anna-Carnations in the garden of the Hietzing villa.

Uncle Emmerich

My uncle Emmerich had no heart. He speculated on copies of old paintings billed as originals, which, in some cases, later actually turned out to be originals. But finally he went bankrupt. We boys were present at the dinner table on the eve of the "Economic Capitulation in the House of Emmerich," at which my uncle argued, based on irrefutable evidence in Silberer's *Sports News*, his bible, that "Quick Four" was bound to win at the big race on Sunday. Aside from which, he got private tips to that effect from the stable. All of a sudden he looked up and noticed that his wife and daughter were quietly weeping. "Will somebody please tell me why in heaven's name these dames have started bawling?" he said. Of course they started bawling because of the lost money. What else do women bawl seriously about? Quick Four didn't win either, neither Quick nor Four, nor in any combination, and my uncle drove home deep in thought on the upper level of the elegant English double-decker sports omnibus (at ten Crowns a seat), armed with the very same binoculars likewise employed by Count Niki Esterhazy. "There goes the dowry of our poor daughters!" my aunt kept weeping. "Teach your child not to need a dowry!" said my uncle. When he auctioned off his collection of paintings, for which he had been derided all his life by the family, it turned out that it had been worth more than all the money he'd squandered otherwise. Henceforth, the family, which had previously called him a dimwit, called him a remarkable man. And my aunt said: "Emmerich, in your heart of hearts you're a good man after all!"

My Aunt

I have an aunt. My first memory of her is as follows: My uncle offered a toast at the wedding dinner. At that very moment I had in my mouth two candied strawberries, a chocolate praline with coffee filling, a hazelnut pâte and a pineapple fondant complete with paper wrapping. Then my father said: "You see...!?" He was referring to the quote from Goethe with which the toast concluded. You see how nice it is when you know something, you're heaped with honors and on top of it all you even get a bride.

In truth, I saw that such knowledge could get you a rather skinny and not very good looking bride. At the end of the dinner I saw my uncle standing with her beside a yellow silk damask curtain, probably saying to her: "Let me conclude with the wise words of Goethe...," whereupon my aunt could not help but get an eyeful of the bizarre pattern of the damask curtain.

Very soon after these events my aunt became fat and my uncle wrote a book about the national prosperity. I only knew that my aunt could laugh like a fool, for instance, if someone said: "You know how Mr. Z. walks, don't you?! He walks like this..." Then she shook herself out laughing and her arms became very short and fat and vibrated with merriment. My uncle considered everything "from the standpoint of a national economist—." He felt: "The thinking of a man of genius revolves around a set point, taking all sides into consideration; these, for instance, are the counter-arguments—."

"How Clotilde can laugh...!" the ladies remarked at high tea.

"Indeed," said one, "her husband considers it a savings for the GNP, you get more out of nutritious matter, digest it all; laughter is healthy. Grief—a waste of vital strengths, joy—a savings! It's all a chain reaction."

A young girl said: "I think her laughter is a kind of crying; it's pretty much the same... only in reverse..."

"Don't talk such nonsense," they said to the young girl. "You're already ditzy enough."

One night I met my aunt with her daughter at a ball. She had on a red silk gown, was very fat and looked just like a mortadella sausage. The daughter hobnobbed with millionaires' sons with noble "vons" tacked onto their names and decked out in snow-white tails with gold buttons.

My aunt said to me: "Say, I want to tell you something, come with me . . . !"

She led me down the halls.

She stopped in one room.

"That's it . . . ," she said, "will you take a look at her . . . !"

Seated there was a strawberry blonde American girl who looked like an angel and like the heavens and all the flowers in the field!

My fat aunt and I just stood there . . .

My aunt, the mortadella sausage, folded her hands and whispered quietly: "God protect her!"

I led her back . . .

She was altogether flustered. "I beg you," she said, "don't breathe a word of this to my husband or my daughter, I just showed her to you because you're so crazy . . ."

I looked her in the eyes and said: "Of course . . ."

Then she said: "Will you get a load of the high-class boys my daughter's hobnobbing with . . . ?!"

"Pst," I said, "from the standpoint of the national GNP . . ."

"Indeed," she said, "but I also want Elsie to marry well, rich and happy . . ."

"Of course . . . ," I said, "are you happy, Auntie?"

"I'm too fat and too crazy for happiness . . . ," she said, "but that's between me and you."

"To the last point at least I can attest . . . ," I said, whereupon my aunt exploded in laughter.

Career

The press photographer who was supposed to photograph two walls of my room because "the big European illustrated magazines" wanted to give their eager readers a glimpse of P.A.'s digs, said: "I'd like to include in the picture a piece of your desk." — "That's altogether unnecessary, since, first of all, I don't have a desk, and second, I do all my writing in bed. Why don't you include a bit of my bed!" — I said: "So how do you become a press photographer? I only know how you become a poet. You're a disgrace to your kind-hearted parents, a failed lawyer, doctor, book dealer and then nothing at all. But how do you become a press photographer?!"

The man wrinkled his brow into deep pleats — I never actually observed this happen, before or then and there, but since they put it that way in novels — and began: "I had a voice, bass, baritone and tenor all rolled in one!"

"Must one have that if one wishes to become a press photographer?"

"I had a voice! Opera director Herbeck, who happened to be in the audience incognito, approached me and said: 'Go to Gänsbacher tomorrow, sing him what you sang today, he'll give you lessons, there's no fee!' I had no idea who Herbeck was, Gänsbacher either. Only my father wept tears of joy and my mother said: 'I always knew it!' (It's a mother's job to know everything in advance when things happen after the fact and the father's iron severity melts into hot and discrete tears at the first sign of some 'success.') Gänsbacher said to me: 'Damn good!' After the seventeenth lesson I took a trip to Luxembourg, and when, all sweaty from rowing, I sneezed in the skiff, a chilly gust blows by and I lose my voice. The next day Gänsbacher said to me: 'Get lost and don't you ever come back. You're done!' My mother said she saw it all coming, and my father said: 'You're a shirker through and through.' Well, so then I went and became a press photographer. And, believe me, I'm just as happy as I was with that stupid singing!"

The Bed

Your bed is wonderful, a kind of refuge from the perils of waking life! But also a peril in and of itself—a kind of pre-casket, that is, in preparation for your passing. In bed your life absorbs obstructive strengths, all that which is supposed to hold back your demise lets go! Only outside your bed are you actually able to resist the thousand hostile forces of your life! In bed you are inescapably prone, decayed, and you yourself decay. Your bed shelters your preexistent store of strengths, but simultaneously hinders access to the new strengths to be derived from the fluid life of day! You withdraw yourself from the useful fight. Your bed is a kind of pre-casket! It is death in life! A soft death that permits a rising. But never forget it, grownup: children in the cradle, invalids in bed sleep endlessly long! That simply means they're not yet up to living. Or else they'd tolerate "the waking state." The waking man lives, the sleeper has died!

You can make amends for many sins with ample sleep—. But what if you commit none? Your bed is your pre-casket. As soon as you fall asleep in it, some precious thing or another perishes in you!

Celebrity

We were once a large group of artists in a champagne pavilion at "Venice in Vienna" in a summer wine garden. Three sweet young girls immediately joined us. Someone in our group told them: "Girls, don't you know in whose company you have the honor of being seated today? That gentleman over there happens to be the famous painter Gustav Klimt!"—"You don't say—," the girls replied nonchalantly. Then a fourth girl joined them and said: "Girls, do you know who that is?! It's him, no doubt about it—." "Aw, what's the big deal, who could care less whoever he is—." —"But that's the guy who paid for twelve bottles of Charles Heidsieck champagne at the Casino de Paris last winter!"—"No kidding, is that really him?! Right! Now I recognize him! Hey, Mr. famous painter, here's lookin' at you!"

P.S. The local representative of Charles Heidsieck champagne once said to me at a late hour: "Say, Peter, I was just wondering if you could ever include my company in one of your sketches? In which case, Peter, you can swig as much as you like!"

Now I hope with some justification to drink my fill. By the way, that time with Klimt & company, it wasn't Charles Heidsieck we were drinking, it was Pommery. But since the one is just as good as the other, and besides, we still get to drink on it, who cares?!

Poem

I hired a girl for the night.
   So what.
   Before she fell asleep she said: "Are you a poet?"
   "Why? Could be. So what."
   "I once made up a poem myself—."
   "?!?"
      "How dear to me you are.
      Now you're so far—.
         So what.
      Let 'em write on my gravestone:
         'I love you alone!'
      Nobody will know who and whom—.
         So what."
   I gave the girl ten Gulden instead of five—.
   "Oh," she said with a smile, "five is all we agreed on."
   "So what. My calculation's on the mark. Look here, my girl,
how precisely I tally—
   five for your sweet body and five for your sweet soul!"

Love

He loved her desperately and in vain. You always only love desperately when it's in vain! Then she fell very, very ill. So she said to him: "I feel pity for you. I want to show myself to you more naked than naked!" And she unrolled a large sheet of paper on which her x-ray had been printed. "Oh, what a darling little skeleton!" he said, delighted. "But I beg you this one favor, just don't go and show it to Mr. —; that much advantage I'd at least like to have over that dog!"

Theater Evening

She couldn't take the poodle with her into the theater. So the poodle stayed with me in the café and we awaited the mistress.

He stationed himself so as to keep an eye on the entrance, and I found this very expedient, if a bit excessive, since, honestly, it was only half past seven in the evening and we had to wait till a quarter past eleven.

We sat there and waited.

Every carriage that rattled by awakened hope in him, and every time I said to him: "It's not possible, it can't be her yet, be reasonable, it's just not possible!"

Sometimes I said to him: "Our beautiful, kind-hearted mistress —!"

He was positively sick with longing, twisted his head in my direction: "Is she coming or isn't she?!"

At one point he abandoned his guard post, came close to me, lay his paw on my knee and I kissed him.

As if he'd said to me: "Go ahead, tell me the truth, I can take anything!"

At ten o'clock he began to whine.

So I said to him: "Listen pal, don't you think I'm antsy? You've got to control yourself!"

But he didn't put much stock in control and whined.

Then he started softly weeping.

"Is she coming or isn't she?!"

"She's coming, she's coming —."

Then he lay himself perfectly flat on the floor and I sat there rather stooped over in my chair.

He wasn't whining any more, just stared at the entrance while I stared ahead of me.

It was a quarter to twelve.

She came at last. With her sweet, soft, sliding steps, she came quietly and collected, greeted us in her mild manner.

The poodle whined, sang out and leapt.

But I helped her off with her silken coat and hung it on a hook.

Then we sat down.

"Were you antsy?!" she asked.

As if one said: "How's life, my friend?" or: "Yours truly, N.N.!"

Then she said: "Oh, it was just wonderful in the theater—!"

But I felt: Longing, longing that flows and flows and flows from the hearts of man and beast, where do you go?! Do you perhaps evaporate in the heavens like water in the clouds?! Just as the atmosphere is full of water vapor so must the world be full and heavy with longings that came and found no soul to take them in! What happens to you, dear emotion, the best and most delicate thing in life, if you don't find willing souls greedy to soak you up and derive their own strength from yours?

Longing, longing, that flows from the hearts of man and beast, flooding, flooding the world, where do you go?

Poverty

Conversation with my ten-year-old dinner guest, Karoline B., the little daughter of a poor widow, perfection in the making, already a profoundly human creature.

"Tomorrow, Sir, I have to travel far out to the 'Doll Doctor' in the Fifth District!"

"What ever for?"

"Somebody gave me a doll. She only has a top half."

"Curious!"

"Why curious?! If she'd had a bottom half, too, they damn sure wouldn't have given her to me!"

The Little Silk Swatches

I wrote to the department store G.: "For the last few days my heavenly little thirteen-year-old friend with the ash-blond hair, the light gray eyes and the black lashes has been spreading out for my perusal eight to ten homely little swatches of silk on a patch of grass all gray from the dust of automobiles, saying: 'Which is the prettiest?! The gray one with the lilac-colored threads, don't you think—.' I asked her what all these little swatches were about, whereupon she replied: 'They're hard to get. This girlfriend of mine, she's got a sister who works for a tailoring outfit in Vienna. And my friend left me ten of her best samples, 'cause we're real pals, see. But we tell the other girls they're only rags to wipe the ink off pens. 'Cause if them other girls knew that they were good for nothing and we just like 'em, that's all, they'd be so sad that they didn't have any—.'" In response to the above, the department store G. sent me a big box full of the loveliest silk remnants, little silk swatches, particularly pretty Japanese and Indian patterns, for my thirteen-year-old friend. That evening, ten schoolgirls gathered in a circle on the lawn, in the center of which, enthroned, as it were, on the box, my fanatically adored little friend, a shoemaker's daughter, held court. She picked up every little swatch of silk and passed it around the circle to each of the stunned girls struck dumb with amazement. The oldest girl said: "Can you really buy enough material of each little rag to make yourself a whole dress?"— "What for, you silly goose, aren't the rags much nicer just as they are?" replied my heavenly little thirteen-year-old. The automobile dust of the rich enveloped lawn and lane in a thick white fog, while the clouds were pierced by blood-red zigzags from the setting sun. Whereupon my friend shut the box and said: "End of silk swatch show for today, ladies and gentlemen—," hoisted the box onto her dear little ash blond head and said to me: "Tonight I'll sleep tight and dream sweet sweet dreams, but not of you, no Sir, I'm going to dream about your wonderfully lovely little swatches of silk—!"

Day of Affluence

I wanted just once for a half day to live the life of a rich man. I arranged to have myself picked up at my place by a ravishing lady and her husband in their Mercedes. I was driven to my barber, on Teinfaltstrasse, to rejuvenate myself, especially with a splash of the menthol-scented French brandy cologne on the head. An ersatz for any cold bath! Then we drove to Baden. There we took baths in the Kurhaus private tubs, 24 degrees Celsius. Then we had them unlock cool hotel rooms and slept for a good half hour. Then we ate Solo asparagus and fricasseed calves' brains. Then we drove on to Heiligenkreuz. In a cool hall we sipped steaming hot tea with lemon. We dashed back home in the evening.

The meadows wafted sweetly and the forest stood black and motionlessly melancholic beneath the still light of the evening sky.

In Vienna I said goodbye.

Seated in the Café Ritz I spotted that young woman whom I have long found pleasing to look at. Brown hair, blue straw hat, upturned nose. I wanted to bring the day to a festive conclusion. So I sent her three wonderfully dark roses and an egg punch, the favorite drink of most women of her kind. She graciously accepted, exceptionally.

Then she came over to my table and said:

"Does it really give you such a great pleasure to pay your respects to me?"

"Yes, indeed, or else I wouldn't do it!"

"Well, then, I don't even have to thank you for it—!?"

"No, not at all, the pleasure is all mine!"

That was my day of affluence.

Traveling

There's one dirt cheap pleasure I know that's altogether free of disappointments, to study the train schedule from mid-May on and pick out the very train with which you would, if only . . . So, for instance, at 8:45, you're already up and about and even shaved (to travel unshaven is only half a pleasure, better, if need be, to go without washing); so at 8:45 with the southbound express to Payerbach, and from there by one-horse carriage (my favorite driven by Michael Ruppert, Jr.) to the heavenly idyllic Thalhof Hotel. Once there you do nothing at all for the moment, seeing as you're actually still seated in your room in Vienna poring over your travel plans. Enough, everything's fine as it is, facing the forest, the cowshed, the horse stable, the bubbling trout brook, the laundry yard, the woodshed, where once, thirty years ago, with Anna Kaldermann—you gathered wood, and in the distance the hills near the Payerbachgräben where my father wanted to acquire a plot of land planted with sour cherry trees to flee to the holy refuge of nature, while my mother said: "Not until our two daughters are wed, my dear!" So there you sit before your travel plans, 8:45 departure time, dreaming sweet dreams free of the burdens of reality, and you just saved, conservatively speaking, at least twenty Crowns. For every change of place taxes the cost of your stay!

In the Volksgarten

"I'd like to have a blue balloon! A blue balloon is what I'd like!"

"Here's a blue balloon for you, Rosamunde!"

It was explained to her then that there was a gas inside that was lighter than the air in the atmosphere, as a consequence of which, etc. etc.

"I'd like to let it go —," she said, just like that.

"Wouldn't you rather give it to that poor little girl over there?"

"No, I want to let it go —!"

She lets the balloon go, keeps looking after it, till it disappears in the blue sky.

"Aren't you sorry now you didn't give it to the poor little girl?"

"Yes, I should've given it to the poor little girl."

"Here's another blue balloon, give her this one!"

"No, I want to let this one go too up into the blue sky!" — She does so.

She is given a third blue balloon.

She goes over to the poor little girl on her own, gives this one to her, saying: "You let it go!"

"No," says the poor little girl, peering enraptured at the balloon.

In her room it flew up to the ceiling, stayed there for three days, got darker, shriveled up and fell down dead, a little black sack.

Then the poor little girl thought to herself: "I should have let it go outside in the park, up into the blue sky, I'd've kept on looking after it, kept on looking —!"

In the meantime, the rich little girl gets another ten balloons, and one time Uncle Karl even buys her all thirty balloons in one batch. Twenty of them she lets fly up into the sky and gives ten to poor children. From then on she had absolutely no more interest in balloons.

"The stupid balloons —," she said.

Whereupon Aunt Ida observed that she was rather advanced for her age!

The poor little girl dreamed: "I should have let it go up into the blue sky, I'd've kept on looking and looking —!"

Marionette Theater

The old man came home from the puppet theater with his granddaughter Rosita.

He was crab-red. With his white hair on top of his head, it was really spring in winter.

"What a shame not to have seen that — !" he said and gave a sidelong glance at Rosita.

"Of course I would've loved to have come along," said the pale young mother, preparing potato salad with vinegar, holding up the two little yellow bottles to the light so as to tell them apart. Nobody in the world can tell oil and vinegar apart. Someone always says: "Well, what do you think, this must be vinegar." — "That one?! No way," one replies.

"I'd've loved to have come along. Honestly I would. But you and Rosie, you're like two love birds! And such exaltation! Incidentally, Rosie, how was it?"

"I was at a theater — ."

"Yes, and — ?!"

"And I was at a theater!"

"What a little ninny — !"

Whereupon Peter A. replied to the lady: "I was at a theater! That says it all. Need anything more be said?! She expressed herself like a genius. My sweet! My precious! My gentle one! No more need be said: I was at a theater!"

"Go to your Peter, he understands you," said the lady, happy and proud, and let the child down from her lap. Then she cut the meat into little pieces for Rosita. "Do you want potato salad or green peas?"

"First salad — ."

"Didn't she need to go?!" asked the lady.

"No," replied the old man, "we took care of everything beforehand."

The lady sat there, both her arms hanging limp at her sides. She thought: "I saw him again this afternoon, the bane of my existence, Edgar! Oh, what a cad he is. That's how absinthe must affect you. It shatters the nervous system. It's like an obsession of the soul. A symptom of derangement. Instead of being free, to be bound! That's it. He creeps up on my life and binds it! I should have gone along with my child—."

The grandfather sat there, crab-red: "You should've seen Rosie today—! You're such a fool, Hanny. Always worries, errands—."

The old man was beaming with love, drunk with love, the gift of youth, and nameless bliss, forgetting. He was like a minstrel playing the lute to the beautiful wonderful world full of many curling destinies liable to unravel at a gust of spring wind. He felt: "My daughter's stuck in a mediocre marriage, always preoccupied, critical of everything. So what?! Rosita came out of it!"

Rosie sat on Mr. Peter's lap. He softly kissed her golden hair.

"Eljén!" she said and raised her glass to him.

"Who always does that?!" said the lady.

"That one over there!" said Rosita and pointed to the old man.

"Dear, sweet, most gentle one—," said Mr. Peter and pressed her softly to him.

"Did you already thank your Grandpa?" the lady asked, annoyed, "probably not!"

"Yes, I did—. No, I didn't yet."

Mr. Peter kissed her silken hair. He felt: "Who does she need to thank?! We need to cover her little hands with kisses, because she gives and gives and gives us so much. The old man is crab-red all over with gratitude for her gifts and I myself am warm in my heart."

The old man felt: "Thank me?! Oh God."

"Go on, thank him," said the lady who was obsessed with the bane of her existence as with the devil and couldn't get things straight. "A young love," the unconcerned call it, "a fling of the past." But for the concerned parties, it eats its way under your skin like a bark-beetle, tunnels its way through the marrow, undermines, causes collapse. The victim is by no means free. Pressed by himself.

"Say thank you, won't you?!"

These words "say thank you, say thank you, say thank you—" were like shots fired in peacetime. The Hell with "say thank you."

Like a ghost it reared up. It had no substance. Only bones. Always this lie "say thank you." It makes everyone ill at ease.

"Hush now!" said Mr. Peter to himself, "better keep your mouth shut!"

To Rosita he said: "Whisper it quietly into his ear."

"Grandpa, I have to whisper something in your ear."

The old man heard nothing but "ps ps ps ps ps —."

He was all embarrassed. On top of which it tickled him. Not a single word of thanks.

The mother said: "That's a fancy little miss. I don't know what's to become of her. Always taking and taking and taking. Who's going to tolerate that?!"

"The old man and the poet!" replied Mr. Peter and pressed the dear little one softly against himself. Then he said, hard and out-right aggressively: "The rich ones! Those who no longer need to beg on the road of life, the full ones who have stored up the warmth and can radiate it like the sun, those with independent souls who no longer need to whine for love like little children whining for milk and quiet, the grownup rich ones able to do without pitiful taking, the kings, yes, the kings who live on giving! You see, we're crab-red with love!"

The young woman thought: "You've got to be old or mad. But we stayed too young. Is it any fault of ours? We still soak up the juices like a sapling. We rob nature just to exist. Oh and by the way, the earth still has a molten middle, and its chimneys sometimes spew forth and bury places blossoming with life. Isn't that so? Bane of my existence, fire of my soul, Edgar, my beloved, you keep me young, don't let me grow old!"

Everyone sat in silence.

"Rosie, don't be rude. You're going to get too heavy for Mr. Peter. Better go to bed. I'd say you've had yourself a lovely day."

"Where were you today?!" asked Mr. Peter.

"I was at a theater!"

"Where were you?!" he said, because he wanted to hear it a hundred thousand times.

"At a theater!"

"Good night, my dear life," said the crab-red man with the white hair and got all ga ga.

Rosie undressed with the door wide open, stood there all naked, pulled on her nightgown, lay down in her little bed and immediately fell fast asleep.

Everybody sat there in silence. The arms of the young woman hung limp at her sides.

Peter A. felt: "Life, I bow to you! Endowed with two eyes, two ears, Emperor that I am!"

The old man sat there crab-red. He said: "No, anybody who didn't see that child today—"

The lady felt: "Bane of my existence, Edgar! Rosita should have been your child! Yours, do you understand?! Yours and mine!"

She said: "What would become of Rosita in your company, the both of you?! It's a good thing we're going away soon. All these changes. Passing her from hand to hand. It's no good for children. Debauchery."

The two old men were embarrassed like schoolboys.

Mr. Peter eyed the young woman: "Restless one! What are you missing? Always stern and measured in your manner. Never a whimsy." Then he took the little silver spoon that had had the honor of being in Rosie's mouth and pressed it to his lips.

The grandfather got all flustered. People only understand their own poetry. The young woman smiled with glee: "You really are a madman. I'd like to be like you, Mr. Peter, a free-wheeling soul!"

Rosie dreamed in the room next door: "Ohohoho! I was at a theater!"

The old nanny thought: "How restlessly she sleeps. All these frivolities. Imagine, dragging her along to a theater, food for the heart. Children need order. Madame is sensible, not such a lunatic. But who bears the brunt of it all? Me."

At Buffalo Bill's

When she turned 18, she was once asked why she remained so cool and distant to all her charming gentleman callers?

Whereupon the ravishing beauty replied: "I was ten years old. And I went with my beloved Papa and the poet one evening to see Buffalo Bill.* Papa and the poet were very kind to me, and I found myself in an extraordinary state of mind. The whole place was drowned in the shimmer of spotlights and a cloud of pistol smoke, and the American buglers blared through the speedy charges. Everything was out of this world. It lasted for almost three hours, and Papa wanted to take me home with him already before the final number. Then the poet said: 'Elizabeth must not miss the three Circassian riders —.' And so we stayed. Like a storm wind they came sweeping in, astride in their shortened stirrups, their arms spread wide, no reins in sight, unbelievably free and proud, as if hovering on flying horses. I leapt up from my seat, and shivering, grasped Papa's hand. Since then, no one really appeals to me —."

---

*In 1890, Buffalo Bill (Colonel William Cody) brought his Wild West Show to Vienna

Saint Martin's Island

When the doctor gave her the news, that she stood balanced before the dark gates of Tuberculosis, she said: "No way, not at 18 years old, for cryin' out loud!"

And she hurried off to Gravosa,[1] and lay all by her lonesome on Saint Martin's Island with her stock of provisions from 7 A.M. to 7 P.M., and stretched out her arms, naked as the day she was born, to receive the healing energy of nature.

She had her body rubbed with mentholated French brandy twice a day for a good half hour and swallowed a liter of cacao with six raw beaten egg yolks and copious amounts of saltwater fish filets.

When she got well she was full of ambition and a lust for life and she found an engagement acting in a very small theater. Her first role was that of the French Countess Laborde-Vallais. She had no idea what to do with it, but a young gentleman sent his visiting card to her dressing room.

She had bravely plucked herself from the jaws of death and soon realized that life wasn't worth having struggled so mightily to save. She had eluded that peril "Death," — and now had to face the greater peril "Life!" Sunbaths, cacao, beaten egg yolks, mentholated French brandy rubs were not enough to elude life!

Later she happened to make the poet's acquaintance. She didn't understand what it meant to be a poet. You write books and you're a poet. But what's it all about and what good is it?

But one day he said to her: "What was it like on Saint Martin's Island? You lay there, gave yourself to God, and awaited the healing powers of meadow, forest and sunlight — ."

And somebody said to her: "Enough already with your boring Saint Martin's Island! That was then, this is now, thank God!"

Then she peered at the poet with a look that begged for help and he flashed her a helpful look in reply — .

That's when she fathomed what a poet was and what he was good for.

---

*The harbor of Dubrovnik, in Croatia

The Kingfisher

The kingfisher was already ever since childhood my favorite bird.

This contrast between "delicate bird" and "stark winter chill"!

On top of which he's iridescently tinged blue-green like a hummingbird in the tropical forests! The winter hummingbird!

His sharp pointed beak spears little fish out of the water; like harpoons spear whales!

He sits on the lookout for days on end, perched on a tree stump beside a pond. Suddenly he shoots forward, dives under, and spears. An elegant killer.

He robs the carp ponds clean of fish. Nobody would put it past him. For days on end he waits on a tree stump, tinged green-blue, his beak a lance, a sword, a dagger, a fatal needle!

A "romantic retainer" decked out in blue-green iridescent armor! A fairy-tale hero of nature!

Lilly had a pond dug on the grounds of her grandfather's estate, had it bordered with willow, alder, hazel shrubs, oleaster. She had the whole thing caged in by a fine chain-link fence. And she put in a kingfisher. And now she watches him for hours on end roosting and waiting. The master of the pond!

Consequently, the compliments of the gentlemen callers who hope to subdue her delicate soul all sound vapid and laughable.

She is consumed, consumed by the laws of nature and by its mysteries —.

In contrast to which, every man appears petty and pitiful. He's nothing but a "fumbling, brutal, uncomely" kingfisher. He too waits hours, days on end, to trap his prey! He spears and devours. But it isn't "measly minnows" that he devours, slays! He slays "souls"!

The Drummer Belín

He sat with his young wife at "Ronacher's" Variety Show. He said to people who raised their eyebrows: "Why not? I'm interested in the tendrils of art. Aren't there also, after all, perfectly legitimate joints at the Prater? Well then!?"

The show begins at eight o'clock. A thousand bulbs light up.

"The Pickwicks." Fat fellahs in light blue undershirts leapfrog over each other, sweating.

You can almost hear their lungs cry out: "Enough already, cut it out —."

Everybody applauds. The young woman thinks: "Such tiresome — un-wholesome stuff!"

A little girl thin as a pink thread works her way across a white telephone wire.

A thin thing struggling with a thinner thing!

"Unwholesome!" mutters the young woman.

Three bears out of the wild make their appearance. One intones something in his native growl. Nobody understands. It means: "I was wild, wild arggggggggh I was wild —!"

Everybody applauds.

"Thoroughly un-wholesome!" the young woman thinks to herself.

A pantomime up next, "La Puce." "The very soul of silence enveloped by vulgarity."

"A young woman in a light green silk dress undresses herself in search of 'la puce' (the flea), and so misses her rendezvous. The flea is her noble protector. The flea wins the day. Hurray for the flea —!"

Everybody applauds.

The young woman feels: "How terribly tiresome —!"

Now the drum virtuoso Belín.

"That's just what we need, a drummer —," somebody says, "hope he's good for a laugh! What can he do? Beat the drum?!"

The audience cries out to him without words: "Hello, Mr. Drummer —!"

A little drum sits askew on a little drum stand.

He comes out in black tails and a white tie. His wavy hair is streaked with gray.

The piece is called "The Battle!":

Rata-tat tat tat tat — from the distance countless troops come running, millions, ever more, ever more, more, more, more. More — ! They sneak, slide, scurry, fly — . Pause.

Defensive salvo — rata-tat! Pause. Rata-ta, rata-ta, rata-ta, rata-ta — ratatat-tat!

The battle sings its song, shouts, shrieks, screams, moans, breathes its last———. Pause. All of a sudden a terrible uproar ———rrrrata-tat rrrrata rrrrata rrrrata-tat tat tat tat tat — trrrrrrrrra! The death struggle of life: "The Battle!"

Hurricane roll!

He rapes the ear, stretches it, rips it apart, shakes it, brakes it, storms into the soul and makes it — tremble! An awful drum-roll, a terrible, unrelenting, gruesome, bloody-eared drum-roll! Won't he stop it?! He won't stop, rrrrata-tat, rattles on, tears your nerves to shreds, rrrata-tat-tat! Roll it! Roll it — !! Rrrrata-tat!

He mops the floor with 'em, mows 'em down, wipes 'em out!

Bang-bang——— bang! Rrrrrrrrrat———. The battle goes dead. Silence.

The man in black tails rises, bows, makes his exit — .

Nobody applauds.

"A wretched drummer — ," you think to yourself, "tears up the drum skin."

"A genius of the wrist flat out — ," remarks an aristocrat in a box seat.

The young woman sits there, pale as can be — .

"You look scared to death — ," says the husband, and lays his hand gently on hers.

"Napoleon — !" she whispers.

"What's that?" says the husband.

"He got so little applause — ," she says, "maybe he'll be fired — ."

"Oh no — ," says the husband, "they're on contract — . How pale you look — ."

The young woman gulps: "Napoleon — !"

Twelve

"Fishing must be very boring," said a young lady who knew as much about it as most young ladies.

"If it were boring I wouldn't do it," replied the child with the dirty blond hair and gazelle-like legs.

She stood there with the great unflinching solemnity of the fisherman. She took the little fish off the hook and hurled it to the ground.

The little fish died — .

The lake lay there bathed in light and shimmering. It smelled of willows and steaming rotting swamp grass. You could hear the clatter of knives, forks and plates from the hotel. The little fish danced around on the ground a short original fandango like the dance of wild tribes — and died.

The child kept on fishing, with the great unflinching solemnity of the fisherman.

"Je ne permettrais jamais, que ma fille s'adonnât à une occupation si cruelle." I'd never let my girl give herself over to such a cruel activity, said an old lady seated nearby.

The child took the little fish off the hook and once again hurled it to the ground, at the lady's feet.

The little fish died — . It lunged upwards and dropped dead — a simple, placid death. It even forgot to dance, gave up the ghost just like that.

"Oh — ," said the old lady.

And yet, in the face of the cruel child with the dirty blond hair you could discern a deepening beauty and the traces of a soul in the making — .

But the face of the noble lady was languid and pale — .

She will no longer give anyone joy, light and warmth — .

That's why she sympathizes with the little fish.

Why should it die when it still has life left in it — ?

And yet it lunges up and drops dread — a simple placid death.

The child keeps on fishing with the great unflinching solemnity of the fisherman. Beautiful beyond description with big, determined eyes, dirty blond hair and gazelle-like legs.

Perhaps one day the child too will pity a little fish and say: "Je ne permettrais jamais, que ma fille s'adonnât à une occupation si cruelle." I'd never let my girl give herself over to such a cruel activity—!"

But such tender stirrings of the soul only burst into bloom at the last resting place of all dashed dreams, all blighted hopes—.

So fish on, lovely little girl!

As, oblivious to all, you still bear your beautiful birthright buried in your breast—!

Kill the little fish and fish on!

Seventeen to Thirty

I once went to the foremost hairdresser in the capital.

Everything smelled of Eau de Cologne, of fresh washed linen and fragrant cigarette smoke — Sultan Flor, Cigarettes des Princesses égyptiennes.

A young girl with light blond silken hair sat at the cash register.

"Dear God," I thought, "a count will surely sweep you off your feet, you lovely thing — !"

She peered back at me with a look that said: "Whoever you may be, one among thousands, I declare to you that life lies before me, life — ! Don't you know it?!"

I knew it.

"Ah well," I thought, "it might also be a prince — !"

She married the proprietor of a café who went bust a year later.

She was built like a gazelle. Silk and velvet hardly enhanced her beauty — she was probably most beautiful in the buff.

The café proprietor went bust.

I ran into her on the street with a child.

She peered back at me with a look that said: "I still have life before me, life, don't you know it — ?!"

I knew it.

A friend of mine had typhus. He was a well-to-do bachelor and lived in a lakefront villa.

When I visited him, a young woman with light blond silken hair prepared his ice packs. Her delicate hands were red and raw from the ice water. She peered back at me: "This is life — ! I love it — ! Because it's life — !"

When he got well he passed the woman on to another rich young man — .

He dumped her, just like that — .

It was summer.

Later he was overcome by longing — it was fall.

She had looked after him, nestled close with her sweet gazelle limbs — .

He wrote to her: "Come back to me — !

One evening in October I spotted her with him entering the wondrous vestibule in which eight red marble columns shimmered.

I greeted her.

She peered back at me: "Life lies behind me, life —! Don't you know it?!"

I knew it.

I went to the foremost hairdresser in the capital.

It still smelled of Eau de Cologne, of fresh washed linen and fragrant cigarette smoke — Sultan Flor, Cigarettes des princesses égyptiennes.

Another girl sat at the cash register, this one with brown wavy hair.

She peered back at me with the grand triumphant look of youth — profectio Divae Augustae Victricis: "Whoever you may be, one among thousands, I declare to you that life lies before me, life —! Don't you know it?!"

I knew it.

"Dear God," I thought, "a count will surely sweep you off your feet — but it might also be a prince!"

Schubert

Above my bed hangs a carbon print of the painting by Gustav Klimt: Schubert. Schubert is singing songs for piano by candlelight with three little Viennese Misses. Beneath it I scribbled: "One of my gods! People created the gods so as, despite all, to somehow rouse otherwise unfulfilled ideals hidden in their hearts into a more vital form!"

I often read from Niggli's Schubert biography. Its intent, you see, is to present Schubert's life, not Niggli's thoughts about it. But I have returned a hundred times to the passage on page 37. He was a music teacher on the estate of Count Esterhazy in Zelesz, an instructor to the very young Countesses Marie and Karoline. To Karoline he lost his heart. Thus emerged his creations for four-handed piano. The young countess never learned of his profound affection. Only once when she teased him that he had never dedicated a single one of his compositions to her, he replied: "What for?! As it is, it's all for you!"

As if a heart about to burst revealed its grief and then closed up again for eternity—. That's why I often turn to page 37 in Niggli's biography of Schubert.

Gramophone Record

(Deutsche Grammaphonaktiengesellschaft.)
C2-42531. *The Trout* by Schubert.

Mountain stream water burbling crystal clear between cliff and pine tree permutated into music. The trout, a ravishing predator, light gray with red speckles, lurking, standing, flowing, shooting forward, downward, upward, disappearing. Beautiful bloodthirstiness!

The piano accompaniment is sweet, soft, monotone of gurgling torrent, deep and dark green. Real life is no longer needed. We feel the fairy tale of nature!

Every day in Gmunden in the afternoon hours, a lady in a watchmaker's shop had them play the gramophone record C2-42531 two to three times. She sat on a tabouret, I stood close to the device.

We never said a word to each other.

Henceforth she would always hold off on the concert till I appeared.

One day she paid to have it played three times, whereupon she was about to leave. I paid to have it played a fourth time. She waited at the door, listened along to the end.

Gramophone record C2-42531, Schubert, *The Trout*.

One day she didn't come any more.

The song survived like a present from her.

Autumn came, and the esplanade was lightly paved with scattered yellow leaves.

And then they shelved the gramophone in the watchmaker's shop since it no longer paid to keep it.

A Real True Relationship

She sat by the immense ground floor window that almost reached down to the ground of the dusty, gray, miserable country lane, and sewed blouses on a lovely, glittering sewing machine from morning to night. Her eyes wore an expression of despair. But she herself was not aware of it. She sewed, sewed and sewed.

She was very slender, not made for the storm of life that shakes and sweeps away souls and bodies. In the evening she ate the cold vegetables from her midday meal. All this I saw through the immense ground floor window and she saw that I saw it all.

One evening she stood leaning against the front door of the house. And she said to me: "I've taken a job in a blouse factory in Mariahilf, so I won't have to work on my own any longer in this lonely room."

And I thought: "Country lane, country lane, you've lost your sparkle, you've lost your riches.

"A person's got to get ahead in life, isn't that so?" she said, "and by the way, I've always watched you walk by my window, three times a day. Three times a day you walked by, that's right. But in Mariahilf there'll be forty girls, and we'll be able to chatter and work like in an anthill—."

"Listen, Miss, I'll still walk three times past your window when you won't be seated there anymore—."

"Will you really?!? Well, then in a way I'll still be there too, I'll be back home just like before—."

"Maybe you could leave your glittering little sewing machine at the window and with it one of your unfinished blouses—."

"Sure, why not, I will—."

That was the only real true relationship I ever had with a female soul in my entire uneventful life—.

Country lane, gray, dusty country lane, so now you've lost your sparkle, you've lost your riches—. And she, she's going to work now, going out into the world—!

The Nature of Friendship

I know two people with true feelings of friendship for me, my brother and A.R. They understand everything I think, feel, say, derive from all these things the rosiest interpretation. They have absolutely no wish to set traps for me. They perceive only the worthwhile, ignore any possible sour notes without blinking. They draw off the cream from the beloved person, don't quibble about the watery milk that floats beneath it, but rather take it as a law of nature that the cream can't reach down all the way to the bottom — . They elucidate us according to our own ideals hidden within, not according to our all too conspicuous everyday failings! They watch for our rare highpoints, turning a blind eye to our depravities. They are noble interpreters, expounders of our true nature. They fathom our frailties, they respect our strengths. They deal with us as one does with purebred canaries, parrots, starlings, dogs, monkeys. One respects their innate character, but demands nothing impossible from them. One holds up their "distinctive" exceptional qualities. This benevolently sentimental form of even-keeled kindheartedness is called: friendship. Any other kind is a sham. This noble "eternal kindheartedness" is a gift of God! It is generally reserved for the dearly departed. Only after death do we fully fathom the distinctive qualities of a loved one, delve deeper into their essence, the living manifestations of which no longer disturb us. So long as he lived he committed the irritating maladroitness to be someone other in his thinking and feeling than ourselves!

October Sunday

A steamy sun-drenched quiet afternoon. I sit and write. Somebody knocks at the door. "Please do not disturb me, I must be alone!"

"Gee, Peter, I really just wanted to chitchat with you, it's so boring today, do you have office hours, are you poetizing?"

"Why the irony? Yes, I'm poetizing."

"But Peter, you're not some kind of manual laborer, thank God you've got no steady job, you can go right back to composing your poetry undisturbed in two hours when I'm gone!?"

"Just try it some time, you don't seem to understand much about this kind of work!"

"That's a new one, a poet who keeps office hours and refuses to receive a friend who'd just like to pleasantly chitchat with him. It's not like your *impressions* are going to evaporate away! Or are they?!"

"Would you ever think of troubling a lawyer, a doctor, a bank director while he was engaged in his work?!"

"Engaged in his work, Peter, come off it, yours isn't work in the ordinary sense of the word, it's a distraction, an amusement!"

"Do you wish to impede my distraction, my amusement with your pleasant *chitchat*?!"

"See you 'round, Peter, you're downright ungrateful to your admirers, but nobody takes you seriously, thank God. Adieu. Poet! I don't want to be the cause of *the world's* missing out on something! So long."

Fellow Man

No one man can abide another, in matters big or small, he just can't do it, that is his eternally unspoken tragedy. He can't give the reasons, which is why he must keep it to himself. That is his tragedy. He has no reason to be unhappy and yet he is, and so must bear it in silence. But when grief finally explodes it generally explodes wrongly and unjustly. Which is far worse. So to "grin and bear it" is the best thing to do. A "flare-up" calls for an immense reserve of spiritual strength and brutality, disregard for others. Who has it?! Who benefits from it?!?

So grin and bear it! Yuck!

Can you possibly know what plagues another, say your fellow man? The fact is, you don't even want to know. What a miserable doddering camel you are, loaded down, burdened with your own intimate woes. Your concern for others is a forced comedy you put on for your allegedly kind heart! Nobody has natural Savior-like inclinations. There is only one. And he got his just due, they finished him off, in fact. Interest?! At best you're interested in yourself and not even that, you're not wise enough to be so farsighted. You lend an ear, but that's the most tiresome thing of all, the fate of others. "Here, take twenty Crowns, but do shut up!" No, better let him get it off his chest — .

The Reader

"The things Altenberg writes, we already know them anyhow!"

Because he writes in such a way as to give you the impression that you've always known it anyhow.

But it's only through him that you know that you've always known it anyhow, that is, ought to have known it!

You're embarrassed in front of yourself, to have fathomed it only now thanks to that crazy eccentric Altenberg!

There's only one way out:

"Well for crying out loud, I already thought that, knew that, long ago, do you have to spell everything out?! That Altenberg fellow is a nut, he has the need to enlighten!"

Do I really?! It's fine with me if the others fumble and falter on their own foolishness.

Modern Diogenes

Why am I unsociable? I'll tell you. Say, for instance, I did not happen to be so, I would surely experience the following every evening at my regular café table where I retire to try and rest up after a hard day of doing nothing: "Do tell us, Peter Altenberg, I'm just dying to know, what's your position regarding the works of Karl Schönherr?!" * First of all, of course, I have no position, and second, if I had a position, I would have no burning need to impart it at 10:45 on the dot after the seventh mug of Pilsner! Or: "Gee, Peter, it's good to have met you in person, one thing I've always wanted to hear from your own lips, this business about women, dames, they always seem to have played a significant role in your life?! Do you really think they matter that much?!" But if you reply: "what matters to me is me and how I experience the various kinds of women!" then he says: "Naturally, you're all swelled heads, you scribblers!"

So now do you understand why I'm unsociable?! To which you'll promptly reply that that's just the way life is! Yes, but in my book it's different!

* Karl Schönherr, 1867–1943, Viennese folk dramatist and doctor

Conversation

Most people live out their life with an almost pathologically bottled up world view. The most insignificant occurrences in their own experience and the experiences of their few acquaintances not only preoccupy their thinking, but such people also unknowingly attempt to derive therefrom deep philosophical problems and universal judgments intended to open up wide-ranging perspectives! "So what are we to conclude from the fact that Anna had to go and buy herself this particular hat?! How are we to take an impartial position?! Is it just a whim, a childish folly, an impertinence, an extravagance, or should somebody in particular perhaps get upset about it?!? That too would be perfectly possible." Everyone attempts with more or less skill to hang his own empty, irrelevant, ridiculous experiences onto the tail end of the conversation underway like a kind of "philosophical-historical" essay, which process one commonly calls "stimulating conversation." "Wouldn't you also agree, despite everything, that G does not really appreciate B quite as much as she rightfully deserves, particularly under such extenuating circumstances?"—"Unfortunately, as much as I would like to, I cannot, 'for reasons of principle,' give you an answer, madam, a principle, moreover, to which you yourself would surely adhere, although in any case a spark of truth appears to flicker forth from your question!" Such is "stimulating conversation!" No one is interested in anyone else, but he "psychoanalyzes" the other because it's "stimulating to dig around behind things and set yourself on a pedestal above them!" The "silent man," the "silent woman" don't come off as wise or decent, but rather boring. "What does he, what does she take him or herself for?" Even the "ironic note" is a rotten dodge in the conversation. Should anyone ever seriously hazard a "fiery stand" in favor of something or other, then, following a brief artificial pause, the firebrand is taken aside: "But surely you couldn't possibly believe that yourself, do you?!?" Conversation is the Moloch that gobbles up and decimates the non-existent spirits and souls! At home one is one's own man, but in society one immediately becomes a philoso-

pher of life in general. Butchers, bakers, busy businessmen, sales-
men do not suddenly transform themselves for hours on end into
"universally thinking" philosophers predisposed to "look down
on the swarming masses of humanity." "It's easy enough to listen
to Altenberg sound off; if it can't help you it can't harm you either,
but that guy, he's one curious customer!" But those that seek to
make us measure up to themselves, to lead us back to the reasonable, salubrious, normal, decent, useful mien, only they make—
conversation with us!

Albert

I received a Crown, dated 1893, the face of which was polished and in which the name "Albert" had been engraved. I immediately felt that in such an unusual case poets had the duty to let their imagination ramble. In any case, it was surely a "she," who, through a circumstance unknown to us, had had this consecrated Crown — perhaps the first lavished on her or the last — so transformed, and in a moment of material need or out of hatred, jealousy, despair, contempt or the like, had sent it back in circulation, back into the current of life, till finally, in 1914, it came to me.

I cherished it for the longest time, and Maeterlinck would have made a one-act out of it: Crown 1893. But when the valet Anton requested payment for cigarettes and I said, at the moment I had no change on hand, he pointed to the 1893 Crown lying on the desk and said: "There's a coin over there!" — "It's invalid!" I said, "just look at it!" — "I'll make do with it, you can count on my dexterity, Sir, nobody'll notice that stupid word "Albert!" And thus did that 1893 Crown slip out of my possession and resume its worldly circulation, which I, in an application of "false Romanticism" had temporarily held up — .

The Private Tutor

At the entrance to the zoo with its black linked metal fence and the ring of dusty lilacs stood a little light brown Swiss chalet glimmering with a fresh coat of varnish baking in the afternoon sun in which the zoo attendant sat chomping on a pear. He sold lemon yellow entrance tickets and dark green reduced price tickets for groups, soldiers and regular visitors. "Les enfants ne comptent pas," he muttered, as if to say: "Go on, get lost, you don't hardly matter — . . ." In a little cage near the sweating Swiss chalet sat two aguti, Dasyprocta aguti.* The cage floor was covered with broken bits of bread rolls and sugar cubes.

A young private tutor with a boy and a girl at his side said: "Stupid people. Fruit is all they eat! Watch this!" He gave them a little peach.

The aguti stood up on their hind legs and ate like chipmunks. The young girl was flushed with admiration and sensed how all the others standing around admired the tutor too or felt a like emotion.

"Remind me, Fortunatina, tomorrow I'll read you in Brehm, all about the favorite live foods of the onza and jaguars of Brasil. These two creatures huddle in the harbor of life. But bread and sugar?! After all, they're not monkeys, par exemple."

Then they went to look at the bears, which lumbering beasts made stereotypical movements and smelled awful and which the public kept egging on to waddle over to the water tank.

"Wait —," said the tutor and tossed an entire bread roll into the tank. Whereupon the bear was compelled to lean in, if only with its upper half.

At the lions' cage, Fortunatina rested her elbows on the wooden railing and looked long and hard. The lioness slunk back and forth, as if slipping on the wet stone floor, as if, alas, creeping up upon some unsuspecting prey?!

The tutor stood back with the boy who wanted to move on: "A lioness, what's the big deal?! She's locked up —."

---

* Sea swine, prevalent in South America

The tutor just stood still.

"Fortunatina and the Lioness —," he thought. He had no idea what it meant, what the story was all about. It was like a ballad which no poet had yet composed. The ballad was there ready to be born in the soul of a poet and set out into the world. Fully formed it fulminated in somebody's head, pressing to see the light of day, wanting to burst into song — Fortunatina and the Lioness!

The tutor just stood still.

The little girl turned to him, blushed, grinned, all flustered, ready to move on.

"There's no shame in dreaming yourself into the souls of animals," thought the tutor. With an understanding smile he lay his wonderful fatherly hands on the shoulders of the child.

Fortunatina dreamed: " — suddenly, in the middle of the night a shriek resounds which, as it were, makes all of nature tremble —. A slash of the claw is just now felling an ox —. There are examples. Africa. Africa. Often in the last minute, cold-bloodedness, decisiveness served the sanguine hunter —."

She peered at her tutor.

But the latter wore wide Pepita-pants, a dark jacket and a small brown felt hat. He also had a walking stick with a deer antler handle and a gold-rimmed pince-nez. He ought to have been standing there bedecked from head to toe in yellow rawhide! Or at least in spats!

They walked on.

You could hear the sound of iron castanets, muffled wooden drums, brass rings chiming.

They came to the dance ground of the Ashantee.

"Syncopated rhythms," said the tutor, "do you hear it?! Tàdă tădàdă dădà tădàdă —."

"Just like the sound of a threshing machine," said the boy.

"Quite right," said the tutor, "syncopes."

"It really does sound like a thresher," said Fortunatina.

"Or like in a train car the sounds you hear rattling below," said the boy.

"Just like in a train car," said Fortunatina. "Somebody really ought to make a music of it with real instruments."

"Bravo Fortunatina —," said the tutor.

"It's music for them in any case —," said the boy.

"Don't rush to make such a big distinction between us and them. For them, for them. What is that supposed to mean?! You think because stupid people set themselves above them, treat them like exotic animals?! Why?! Because their epidermis contains dark pigment cells?! These girls in any case are gentle and good. Come here, little one. *How* is your name?!"

"Tíoko —."

He took the wondrous brown hand and laid it in Fortunatina's hand. The latter became flustered.

Then he took a four-stranded necklace of white glass beads with a gold clasp out of his pocket and gave it to Tíoko.

"Where'd you get that?!" asked the boy, while the girl thought nothing of it.

"Where, wherever!" replied the tutor.

Later the boy said: "You were kind and gentle with Tíoko and you believe that she was the same with you; but it's the opposite."

The tutor peered at him, as if to say: "Stupid person, that's the solution to the riddle of our muddled life." But he said: "Fortunatina, wasn't Tíoko gentle and sweet? You see! She came with us like a faithful companion, never let go of your hand. What pleasure she took in the glass pearls. And in everything else. Her cleanliness, her wonderfully smooth cool skin, her ivory white teeth, her gentle hands and feet, the aristocratic grace of her gait!"

The boy thought: "No matter what he says, he bought her."

Fortunatina said in parting: "Tíoko, I love you."

The boy thought: "Fortunatina makes a big deal out of everything."

The tutor kissed Tíoko.

Fortunatina felt: "They're all gentle, Tíoko, the poor lioness, my tutor. It's just like in paradise, where people and wild animals —."

The boy said: "How much did the glass beads cost? How did you come to have them on you? Go ahead, tell me."

"How come, how come?! You have to open every person's heart with the key that fits that lock."

The boy thought: "Tíoko's a funny one, that's all."

Fortunatina felt: "I want to cry, for Tíoko, for the lioness, for everything."

At the zoo exit the aguti still sat there in their cage, the stupid people kept tossing in bread rolls and sugar cubes. In the light brown varnished little Swiss chalet sat the attendant, still selling lemon yellow entrance tickets and dark green reduced price tickets for groups, soldiers and regular visitors.

"Are you tired, Fortunatina?" asked the tutor.

"A little — ."

"Let's sit down then — ."

There was a bench in a thicket of trees, surrounded by lawns planted with trees. They all felt the pleasant peacefulness, huddled together, as it were. The tutor took a four-stranded necklace of white glass beads with a gold clasp out of his pocket and lay it around Fortunatina's neck.

She trembled with the joy of paradise.

No one said a word.

The boy was all flustered.

"You can smell the grass — ," said the tutor.

They all inhaled the pleasant scent which the earth exhaled from its wondrous lungs, actually from the pores of its skin.

"What will Tíoko do tonight?!" asked the girl.

"She cleans the clothes and shoes, makes the bed, fills the wash-basin with water for the zoo attendant you saw at the entrance."

"I took her for the daughter of the king!"

The tutor kissed her gently on her blond head.

"I have a regal piece of jewelry on," she felt, "like Lady Dudley, four strands of immaculate pearls, priceless, maybe worth four million — ."

The late afternoon earth-lawn gave of its steamlike, foglike freshness to the tired people seated on the hard wood bench, and to the couples in hidden corners of the park who longed for dark and silence. The thickets of trees stood like clouds over the firmament of the lawns. Tíoko trembled back in the zoo, draped the thin heliotrope-colored calico wrap over her wondrous brown breasts that ordinarily hung free and lovely as God made them, granting the noble eyes of men a picture of earthly perfection, an ideal of vitality and the blossoming of life.

Then she crouched on a little wooden stool and peeled potatoes for supper.

"What is Tíoko up to?!" thought the child on the bench.

The tutor held her white hand in his, his wonderful brotherly hands—.

"Allons—," said the boy, "it's awfully boring here and we'll catch a cold. Fortunatina is bound to start sniffling soon."

"Do me a favor, don't worry about it, will you, please, if you please—," said the tutor. They all went home ill at ease and in silence.

On the way, the little girl said to her tutor: "I could very well have caught a sniffle. Are you mad at Oscar?!"

"Dear one, sweet one—," said the tutor and pressed her little hand to his heart.

Conversation with Tíoko

"It's cold and very damp out, Tíoko. Rain puddles everywhere. Your people are naked. What are these thin linen things?! Your hands are cold, Tíoko. I'll warm them for you. At least they could give you cotton flannel, not these threadbare linen rags."

"We're not allowed to dress, Sir, no shoes, not even a head cloth. 'Take it off,' says the attendant, 'take it off. What are you trying to be, some kind of society lady maybe?!'"

"Why doesn't he let you dress?!"

"We're supposed to represent savages, Sir, Africans. It's completely crazy. We'd never go around like this in Africa. Everybody would laugh at us. Like 'bushmen,' that's what they look like, that lot. Nobody lives in huts like these. Back home they'd be fit for dogs, *gbé*. Quite foolish. They want us to be like animals. What do you think, Sir? The attendant says: 'Hey, we've got plenty of proper Europeans already. What do we need you for?! Of course you've got to be naked.'"

"You'll all get sick, you'll die —."

"Oh, Sir, at night we set up little tin containers with glowing charcoal in our huts. Oh, it's so nice and warm. And Manomba's body is warm, I press up against her. And Akolé is warm, and little Dédé is very warm at night. Maybe the sun will shine tomorrow. Then things will be good for Tíoko."

"Tíoko —— !"

"Sir —?!"

"Tíoko ——."

"Do you think, Sir, that the sun will shine warm tomorrow?"

"I hope so."

The Automaton

"Sir—," said the young black man, Mensah, "here in the garden there is a wondrous thing (a mystery). You throw in two Kàple (Kreuzer) and you find out your future."

"Indeed," said Peter A.

"Sir, it's a very crazy thing: In the upper village there is a young Negress whom I love. And she has a husband."

"Does she love him?"

"No."

"How do you know that?!"

"His eyes are too sad."

"Come —."

The gentleman went with the black man to the fortune-telling automaton, which was painted in red lacquer and had a panel with a dial. There where the dial stopped, that was your destiny.

The black man tossed two Kàple in.

The dial turned.

It stopped on the words: "You will take a trip and earn much money unexpectedly."

"Well—?!" said the black man.

"You are loved," said Peter A.

"Sir," said the black man to Peter A. the next day, "can it be known?! There is another such wondrous thing in the garden. If this one says the same thing—!?"

"First show me Méja, your beloved girlfriend."

He took the gentleman to see her.

Méja sat on the dance floor. Her husband came over to her, took off his gray-green woolen pagne and lay it on her delicate shoulders, because the evening wind was just lifting in the garden.

She remained motionless.

"Come —," said the gentleman to the black man.

The blue lacquered automaton worked precisely.

The dial stopped turning.

"Well—?" said Mensah.

"A great misfortune awaits you. But there is still time to turn back. Think it over!" said the gentleman, while the automaton pointed to good luck and love.

Mensah dropped into deep thought —.

"Thank you, Sir."

Pause.

Then said Mensah: "And yet she had such sad eyes —."

But the gentleman thought: "Gently he lay a shawl on her shoulders when the evening wind was lifting —!"

Adultery

"And what consequences does adultery have in your culture, Samson Adukuè?!?"

"How do you mean, Sir?!?"

"Well, does he beat her, send her back to her parents, does he go so far as to kill her?"

"Why ever would he do such things, Sir? He married her because he loves her!"

"But adultery must result in some consequences all the same?"

"Oh yes, Sir, terrible consequences. Until then he had the great love for her, and from then on he only still has the small love!"

Philosophy

Visitors to the Ashanti Village knock in the evening on the wooden walls of the huts for a lark.

The goldsmith Nôthëi: "Sir, if you came to us in Accra as objects on exhibit, we wouldn't knock on the walls of your huts in the evening!"

Akolé

"She's supposed to be the most beautiful," the visitors remark, "a real dish where she comes from. Where the hell is Ashanti anyway?! Not bad for a Negress—. She's a proud one, not very nice. What does she take herself for, the black girl?! Like it's some kind of honor to buy her junk?! Won't even look us in the face when she takes our money for Le Ta Kotsa, tooth cleaning twig. It's a swindle, I tell you. What are you, homesick or something? Our salesgirls wouldn't earn a dime like that. Got to be friendly, sweetheart, nobody's gonna bite you. She's cold, the poor little hophead. Now, now, now, now, don't get upset! Who do you think you are?! Some kind of highborn lady?! Bet you'll give it to me for less. Arrogant slut. Adieu. Can't get anything out of her. Good-bye, black girl, don't go to any trouble now. You're going to be just fine. So long."

"Bènjo, bènjo——!" (The hell with you, get lost!)

Complications

Akolé, lovely like a bust by Barbédienne* cast in bronze, a young man of means wants to possess you!

In your kinky hair you wear the little gold comb he gave you!

He comes driving up in a horse-drawn carriage. His Mother wears a hat bedecked with French violets and greets you, all smiles, Akolé: "It would be an ideal moment in Victor's life, his very salvation. The girl speaks no language. We have her under our thumb. She's ours. I think she likes me. What could she possibly want?! Another string of glass beads and another. And a silk umbrella and sandals. She's black, not everyone's cup of tea, dumb to the world. No complications de l'âme.† I dare say she'd be an ideal moment in his life, medicine for his indolent played-out soul, a veritable tonic. Something special, I tell you, like a trip abroad or a year of military service. Something transformative, exhilarating. Something like an episode in the life of an artist, a poet. Later, well that's another story, isn't it—?!

"Akolé—," says Ofulu Ahadjí, "misumo (I love you)—."

"Akolé—," says Peter A., "return to Akkra—!"

"Akolé—!" says the young man of means who wants to possess her.

The mother says nothing, just plants soft kisses on her forehead—.

---

*Ferdinand Barbédienne, 1810–1892, a caster of bronze replicas of famous sculptures
†Complications of the soul

The Novice Postal Clerk

"It's a somewhat frigid profession—," said the dowdy old postal worker to the very young novice and showed her how to handle the "L.u.C. Hardtmuth" rubber rolling system. "No, romantic it's not in the post office, thank God. We're far removed from the wafting woods—."

And everyone laughed or smiled at least, rather moved.

"When you think," said the very young novice, "that back in the old days they used to have to lick all the registered mail coupons themselves! Was there ever enough saliva?!"

The entire office laughed. Yes, indeed, that's progress for you!

"So," thought the novice, "a frosty profession?! They're all so kind to me. As if I were a convalescent. Nobody wants to hurt my feelings. But am I made of sugar?! They're all so delicate with me, as if to say: 'You too must bear the yoke!' I feel like I'm putting one over on them all. And that other life out there, all boredom and flirtation!? No, thank you, at least now I know what I'm here for. An orderly regulated life! No more unhealthy dreams. Romantic, was it ever romantic at my aunt's house?! Of course there was my gallant uncle making come-on's. No, thank you, I'll take the serious life over that any day."

Hours and hours and hours on end, she wrote out receipts, as if at a gallop, glued yellow stripes, rubber-stamped, tum tum tum tum-pum! Banker's Association: To-in Trieste, to-in Constantinople, to-in Belgrade, to-in, to-in, to-in, tum tum tum tum-pum! At 5 P.M. she received a letter from the gallant uncle. She turned all red in the face and tore it right up. The gall of him!

She galloped onwards over the receipts, hop hop hop höööh-woh!: "Dear girl, if you do it like this, it's much easier." "Thank you kindly."

Many receipt recipients attempted to touch her fingertips. Some even skimmed, as if to stroke, her soft white hand. Only the bank clerks maintained a stony stiffness. Snobs!

Finally she got tired, slowed down to an easy trot, started to pen out her signature in calligraphy.

At 7 P.M., right before closing, a gentleman in a wide coat handed her a letter to be posted registered mail.

"Oh—," said the very young novice, "you've put on much too much postage. West Africa is still a part of the World Wide Postal Union."

She got all giddy over this splendid term "World Wide Postal Union." As if just saying it made her in a certain sense a member of this far-flung family.

"No matter," replied the gentleman, "all the more likely that the letter actually reaches its destination."

"Impractical—," thought the novice.

"What is the lady's name?!" she inquired, as she wished to fill out the receipt.

"Miss Wāh-Badůh."

"In two words?!"

"Naturally."

"A Negress, I suppose."

"Indeed, Miss."

"And in West Africa, Christiansborg?!"

"Yes."

She gave him the receipt with her calligraphic signature.

The gentleman glanced at her, glanced down at her soft white hands and left. In her heart she felt: "A frosty profession?! Not on your life. Like a ride into the land of romance—."

But the dowdy old postal worker observed: "Why do you have to go and tell such a goddamn nut that he put too much postage on?! If the state can't profit off of that sort?! What else are they good for?!"

Conversation with a Chambermaid

"Listen up, my dear Anna, I'm in heaven. An admirer, but not the kind you might imagine, just on account of my books, is going to pay my rent here in town this summer for as long a time as I spend in the country for my really very necessary rest and relaxation."

She turned pale upon hearing this. She thought: "Jesus, there goes my monthly housekeeping tip of six Crowns! If he isn't here then he definitely doesn't need to pay for tidying up the cabinet he even keeps locked up with a Yale lock! He'd be downright batty if he did!"

Whereupon I replied: "Naturally you'll still be paid your six Crowns a month. Why should you have to suffer a loss just because I want a little relaxation in the country?!"

To which she said: "How nicely and comfortably a person could live if there were a lot of people around like you! Why in forty years a person could perhaps even think of retiring! But honestly, Mr. von Altenberg, what's the use if there's just one poet among the many thousands and all the others are such cheapskates?!?"

When my dear and most devoted beloved read this "Sketch from Daily Life," she said: "You see, here you compensate for your absence in the country, but who, pray tell, makes it up to me?!"

Afternoon Break

Chitchat between two stunning young domestics, on their afternoon break, on the fifth floor in the darkened corridor outside my dear little lighted room:

"Jesus, what a fine and fancy broom you've got up here! Ours down in the café kitchen is a sight! Like a plucked chicken!"

"I'll give you mine! Peter'll buy me another!"

"What Peter?!"

"Ya know, Peter. Peter Altenberg. He's a slob, I mean, poor guy, he ain't got nothin', but for practical hardware he's got a heart. Can you believe it, that guy bought a duster for the photographs on his wall, 100% young gray ostrich feathers, it cost him five whole Crowns!"

"Oh, I'd like to get my hands on that one. It must be lovely to wipe with!"

"Yeah, well, that one he don't give to nobody. A hundred times already I must've pleaded with him! He says: 'In my will!' But he's got a good ten years to go. People like that that never lift a finger in their life, except for a little scribbling, they last!"

The Mouse

I checked into the quiet little room on the fifth floor of the good old Stadthotel with two pairs of socks and two large bottles of slivovitz for unseen eventualities.

"If it please, Sir," said the concierge, "shall I have your luggage brought up?!?"

"I have none," I said straight out.

Then he said: "Would you like electric lighting?!"

"Yes."

"It'll cost you fifty Heller a night. But you can also make do with a candle," he said, considering my circumstances.

"No, I'd rather have electric, please."

At midnight, I heard sounds of wallpaper being torn and scratched. Then a mouse appeared, climbed up into the wash basin, made all sorts of curious circular perambulations, and leaped back down to the floor, since porcelain did not suit its purpose. Having no definite, far-reaching plans for the future, it finally found the darkness under the cabinet a rather convenient refuge, under the circumstances.

In the morning, I said to the chambermaid: "Say, last night there was a mouse in my room. That's some clean house you keep!"

"There are no mice in this establishment—that's a good one! Where's a mouse to crawl out of, pray tell?! No one can say such a thing about this hotel!"

After that, I said to the concierge: "Your chambermaid has some nerve. There was a mouse in my room last night."

"There are no mice in this establishment. Where's a mouse to crawl out of, pray tell?! No one can say such a thing about this hotel!"

When I stepped into the hotel lobby, the doorman and the porter looked at me, as did the other two chambermaids and the manager, the way one looks at a person who checks in with two pairs of socks and two bottles of slivovitz and proceeds to see mice that aren't there.

My book, *What the Day Brings*, lay open on my table, and I once caught the chambermaid reading it.

Under these regrettable circumstances, my credibility in regard to mice was rather dubious. On the other hand, however, I did reap the benefits of a certain aura: No one argued with me any longer, they even allowed for little weaknesses to go unnoticed, shut an eye on eccentricities, behaved in an exceptionally accommodating manner as one would with an invalid or a person over whom one takes special pains for some other reason.

Still, the mouse made its regular nightly appearance, scratched at the wallpaper, and often climbed into my wash basin.

One evening, I bought myself a mousetrap complete with bacon, marched ostentatiously with the contraption past the doorman, the porter, the manager, room service, and the three chambermaids, and set the trap in my room. The next morning, I found the mouse in it.

I considered nonchalantly carrying the mousetrap down. The thing would speak for itself!

On the stairs, however, it occurred to me how embittered people become if proven wrong, especially since a mouse is not supposed to be found in a room in a hotel in which "there simply are no" mice! I considered, moreover, that my aura of a man without luggage, with two pairs of socks, two bottles of slivovitz, a book entitled *What the Day Brings*, and who already claims to see mice every night, would, thereby, be considerably shaken, and I would immediately have been relegated to the disagreeable category of complaining and altogether ordinary transient guests. Consequently, I disposed of the mouse in a place rather well suited for such purposes, and once again set the empty trap on the floor of my little room.

From then on I was treated with even greater deference, under no circumstances was I to be upset, and they catered to my needs as to a sickly child. When finally I checked out, my departure was met with the friendliest expression of sympathy and devotion, even though my luggage consisted exclusively of two pairs of socks, two empty slivovitz bottles and a mousetrap!

The Hotel Room

At three A.M. the birds started quietly chirping, suggestively. My worries grew and grew. It started in the brain, as if with a little rolling stone, tore all the joys of hopefulness along with it, the joys that brighten your life, swelled into a sweeping avalanche, burying under the ability to endure the day and the merciless commanding hour! To rise to happenstance! A quiet storm brewed in the branches before my window. For no reason, for absolutely no reason I had burned and bothered the life of sweet Ms. J. And one of my benefactors cut off his modest monthly largesse as of next month. He'd heard something or other about me and my views. They were too radical for him, too uncharitable. My aesthetic ideal, Ms. W., belongs now to those who can pay her. I who pursued the "mystic cult of beauty" was always too inelegantly dressed for her, too incomprehensible and too altogether mad. When I sank to my knees before her, deeply, so deeply stirred by her noble bodily perfection, she said I had perverse inclinations, it wasn't her fault! My hotel room is lighting up, my soul is darkening. Morning is breaking.

The song of the birds in the treetops grows clearer with shreds of simple melody. Quiet storms disseminate the scent of meadows. It would be the perfect hour to hang myself from the window box—.

Elevator

The elevator is still a great mystery to me.

I am not so dumb as to spoil the thrill of the blessings of modern culture by allowing myself to get too accustomed to them!

I still feel it as something wonderful, this secret stair-transcendence, this preservation of my knee joints, of my heart, of my oh! by no means costly time.

The door of my elevator closes slowly, automatically, which proves to be downright annoying to people with packages or baskets, albeit rather pleasant for a writer.

I have no idea by what mechanical devices my elevator dangles. I am merely informed every now and then by the super that something's not quite right today and that the electrical fitter is there. And while I don't understand just what kind of catastrophe was in the making, or what an electrical fitter does, both seem to be linked to a possibly life-threatening situation.

It's awful to ride up with a stranger. You feel compelled to initiate a conversation and obsess on it from one floor to another. You suffer a delayed tension like that of the baccalaureate exam. Your face takes on a frozen glower. Finally you say: "Goodbye!" with a kind of intonation as if you'd just ended a friendship for life. That's why, so as to sidestep all these unpleasantries, I never get home before six in the morning. At that hour the elevator isn't up and running yet.

Visit

He rode up to her in an open cast-iron elevator. It was like a wondrous cage, like a pierced parrot house. Upstairs there was a little white hall with white lacquered walls. The hall wafted with the scent of fine women's garments and Violette de Parme.

The woman stood there in a very small room which was rather warm.

"It really is a little cage—," she said to the man. "Make yourself comfortable. Feel free to smoke—."

"What are you looking at?" she said. "Oh, back into my youth. That one there on the wall is a picture of the room in which I grew up. It's a big homeland, even if it looks very small."

"A big homeland?!" remarked the tattered Tartar.

"That's right. My guardian loved me—. So did his son. His wife's name was Evelyn and she always sat in an easy chair under fruit trees that didn't give off much shade. She only really needed the sun, and the shade of the fruit trees was superfluous. One time she said to me: 'Anita—.' And then she paused. Then she said: 'My husband loves you and my son loves you and I love you. I've never read novels. What's the use of novels? But I'm reading one now and I can't quite get the hang of it.' She expressed herself so sensitively about these complicated matters that were tearing her up inside. No one can explain what happened next. Do you find this boring?! I fled from my guardian, my guiding star, whom I loved, that's right, I fled, even though he wanted to share his life with me. But I held back my life and fled from his."

Pause.

"Are you comfortable in that chair?" said the woman to the tattered Tartar. "You can fetch yourself a pillow. Go ahead, take these white silken ones. It makes no difference."

Then she continued: "After that, the bank director said to me: 'Anita, I love you, I'd like to take care of you—.' 'What for, am I sick—?!' I said. 'Just about—,' he said. So I accepted my gentle caretaker. He protected my somewhat fragile body like a holy thing, so that a soul could blossom in it, a soul that did not always sing his chosen hymns—. The noble man!"

Pause.

"And Evelyn and the son?" asked the Tartar.

"They shriveled up, I think. It may be that they both betook themselves to the fruit trees in the sun and let the dappled shade and sun spots do them in."

"And did the beloved guardian never kiss you?!"

"Of course he did. That's what it was. A guiding star that starts burning instead of glowing! Why did he reject Evelyn, the guardian of us all, our guiding star?!"

The tattered Tartar thought: "Your love sank down to your waistline, Anita, splendid gazelle! You were the very incarnation of my notion of those souls that slip down to the waistline and have to stop here. The soul does not endure the 'sacred transformation' to the bodily, it does not release itself unto the 'blessed delirium,' but, rather, grows and grows into itself and never comes to an end. And finally it transforms you into an impassioned poet who is always enamored of someone, sings sweet hymns and has wondrous dreams. Love is never condensed into the 'physical act,' there is no physical mode of expression, no instrument for the music of living on which the soul could cry itself out, sing its heart out, set itself free! The mystery of 'sexual release' plays no role in the love of the sonorous, self-expressive, self-redemptive soul! Just as the word formed in the throat of the carnal, the sonorous, the revelatory, in the love that flows in bodily release, is a loose translation of the redemptive thought!

"Everything stayed inside you, Anita, and grew inward into the source of mysterious deeds! Of such love a symphony is born, an external score as with the man Beethoven, an internal score for the child-virgin. Never does a little baby blossom from such love, never can you expel it from your tired loins and set it out on your lap as a whole little person. It will always keep welling up and cooling back down again in you in luminous clouds. Woman, you're like a fantastic protoplasm, without the 'holy becoming' and the peace! You're like an artist's soul in perpetual motion, like Beethoven and the sea!"

This is how he expounded upon Anita, traced her back to that place where she came from, her youth!

The woman stood leaning, actually pressing against the white lacquered door, and a faint glimmer of what she had once been hovered over her brown golden hair.

She spoke. She stopped speaking. He spoke. He stopped speaking. She spoke. She stopped speaking—.

It was the second day of the fairy tale of the "stranger who becomes known." The tartar lay in the heap of white pillows and smoked.

Then the woman spoke at greater length, with an exceptionally soft voice, saying: "What are we?! Firewood. Somebody sets us afire, we burn, we give warmth—. But actually we're something that no one knows ——— trees! We're a quiet entity unto ourselves, without any real purpose, like trees in the forest that nobody needs, adorned with leaves and blossoms—. We're something that grows out into the world, into a forest no man has ever tread, a silent wood. The tree had to bend to attain the height that man requires of it, to make little cords of wood cut up for the fireplace. But later, at another time of life, we start to stand upright again and grow, like trees with rustling leaves and stirring branches. Nobody says 'bravo.' It's a forest solitude. Something similar happens on that perfidious night on which nature, that frightful slap-happy force, twists us into a woman. Big, tall, upright, reaching to the heavens, we rear up in childhood and then again much later. Like forest trees that nobody needs with rustling leaves and blossoms—."

She stopped speaking—. They stopped speaking.

And a hundred days went by—. The hundredth day dawned.

He stood up and gave her his hand: "Adieu—."

"Adieu—," said the woman.

She thought: "He looks just like a noble Tartar—.

I revealed my youth to him—! What for?! I made my confession before the fire goes out—."

The little white lacquered hall wafted with the scent of women's garments. The Tartar stood still. He peered down the curl of the black cast-iron stairway and saw at the bottom the wondrous pierced black cast-iron elevator cage, to which three black coils of wire were attached dangling down into an abyss.

He felt: "Anita—." And again he became a mirror for his fellow man, soaking it all up and beaming it back!

And then he thought of the trees in a forest that nobody needs, that grow down into the earth and up into the sky with rustling leaves and blossoms.

And he thought of the people who are not somebody's "pretty object," but rather, like forest trees, great free entities unto themselves with rustling souls and spirit blossoms! And they wilt and sag, like forest trees, and collapse in upon themselves and become humus for the spring. This is how they beget—offspring, life springing off of them! They, the fall that feeds the spring. The tall freewheeling trees in the human forest, the sturdy trunks that won't become chopped firewood, but grow down into the earth and up into the sky! Amen—.

Little Things

For a long time now I've judged people only according to minute details. I am, alas, unable to await the 'great events' in their life through which they will 'disclose' their true selves. I am obliged to predict these 'disclosures' in the little things of life. For instance, in the walking stick handle, the umbrella handle which he or she selects. In the necktie, in the cloth of a dress, in the hat, in the dog which he or she owns, in a thousand unlikely incidentals all the way down to the cufflinks, actually all the way up! For everything is an essay about the person who selected it and gladly dons it! He discloses himself to us! "He wrote a good book, but he wore uncouth, engraved, unnatural cufflinks!" That says everything about him. There's something rotten somewhere in the "state of his soul!" That a beloved lady betray us is not the most important thing. For fate will surely punish her after the fact with profound disappointment! But her first coquettish, fire-kindling glance, that is the salient detail! I can compete with him who betrayed me, absolutely, but not with him who directed a desirous glance in her direction! Little things kill! Fulfillment can always be defeated, but never anticipation! Therefore I hold fast to the little things in life, to neckties, umbrella handles, walking stick handles, stray remarks, neglected gems, pearls of the soul that roll under the table and are picked up by no one! The significant things in life have absolutely no importance. They tell, they make known nothing more about being than we ourselves already know about it! Since when you get right down to it, everything works by and large the same way. But the important differences are only manifest in the details! For instance, which flowers you give to your beloved. Or which belt buckle you pick out for her among the hundred options. Which pear from France, which grapefruit from America you bring to her house, which speckled brown Canada apple you select for her among the hundreds on display; this attests to many more attachments than the orgies of so-called love! Aesthetics, understanding, love must ultimately form a triad. One must be inclined to allow a symphony of ordinary life to resound in the sum of the "little things"! One cannot wait for big events to happen! All the least consequential things are monumental! The squeak of a mouse caught in a trap is a terrible tragedy! Somebody once said to me: the most terrible thing is a young rabbit dragged into a fox hole. The little foxes gnaw at him alive, slowly, day and night, with their needle-sharp little teeth! These are the tragedies of our existence!

Little things in life supplant the "great events." That is their value if you can fathom it!

Idyll

I have a steel-tipped pen rest made of long black bundled bristle set in a light blue shimmering opalized matte glass jar. Protection in an ideal mantel. I think of the Society for the Protection of Children. Something tender, useful, softly and tenderly preserved. I swaddle my ungrudging elastic Kuhn pen like a little child in its cradle, certain that nothing bad will befall it. It dries and rests. And the little glass jar in which the bristle holder sits is an iridescent blue, the color of waves breaking against the sun. And the steel-tipped pen and pen rest return my love, my tenderness, quietly letting it be.

My Ideals

The adagios in the violin sonatas of Beethoven.
The voice and the laughter of Klara and Franzi Panhans.
Speckled tulips.
Franz Schubert.
Solo asparagus, spinach, new potatoes, Carolina rice, salt sticks.
Knut Hamsun.
The intelligence, the soul of Paula Sch.
The blue pen "Kuhn 201."
The condiment: Ketchup.
My little room Number 33: Vienna, First District, Dorotheergasse,
    Graben Hotel.
The good looks of A.M.
Gmunder Lake, Wolfgang Lake.
The Vöslauer * Baths.
The Schneeberg † train.
Mondsee boxed cheese, fresh curdled.
Sole, perch, young hake, reinanken.
Money.
Hansy Klausecker, thirteen years old.

.

---

* Vöslau, a spa near Vienna
† Schneeberg, an Austrian mountain resort

Peter Altenberg as Collector

The *International Collectors News* features an interesting inquiry on the value of collecting in its recently published issue Number 13. The journal includes contributions by, among others, Minister of Education Count Stürgkh, Alfred Lichtwark, Alma Tadema, Harden, Paul Heyse, Max Kalbeck, Eduard Pötzel, Felix Salten, Balduin Groller, Ginzkey. In response to the question as to the why and wherefore of his passion for collecting, Peter Altenberg offered the following intriguing answer: "It's a wonder you should turn to me of all people concerning this subject. Since you could not possibly know that I, a poor man, have for many years been an absolutely fanatic collector and have, just like the millionaires, managed through abundant sacrifices to amass a cherished, painstakingly selected, exquisite gallery of pictures: 1,500 postcards, 20 Hellers apiece, in two lovely Japanese cabinets, each with six compartments. They are exclusively photographic images of landscapes, women, children and animals. Some weeks ago I realized that the truly cultivated individual had to divest himself of his treasures so as to be able to experience while still alive that most profound, that peerless pleasure of 'giving,' of 'bestowing' a thing of value upon a 'beneficiary.' Consequently, I shipped both Japanese cabinets along with the 1,500 postcards collected since 1897 to a young woman in Hamburg, the only one among all women able to appreciate such a present. Since then I've been collecting all the more ardently, all the more passionately, so as to complete my lady friend's collection. — Here then are two healthful deflections from the perilously leaden weight of one's own self: first the pleasure of collecting in and of itself, second the pleasure of being able to do so on behalf of another equally discerning person! 'Collecting' means being able to concentrate on something situated outside the sphere of one's own personality, yet something not quite so perilous and thankless as a beloved woman —."

On the Street
Baudry de Saunier's *The Art of Driving*

Why do all the splendid things conceived, dreamed up by the god-like human brain so soon degenerate into grotesque chicaneries?!? For the very reason that everywhere you look in this earthly existence there's heaven and hell, the deceptive devil and guardian angel side by side!

Nobody who loves the fresh air of nature, the forest and field, the evening and morning, the lazy, easygoing afternoon and the forceful vibrant magnificence before noon, nobody eager to catch a glimpse of a deer in the early evening on the edge of the woods, of hungry crows in a snowy field, of the blossoming and wilting bushes bordering endless streets, the stormy symphonies of mountain streams and the noble, discreet silence of homogeneous groves of trees, nobody so inclined would speed through the world in his holy private luxury automobile and, thereby, endanger his fellow man, animals and himself!

Could you imagine Beethoven, Goethe, Kant speeding along, you men of means?

To let life slowly flow into you, that's all there is to life! Everything else is the pitiful attempt to elude at a speedy clip God's indictment of your failure to grasp the beauties of this world, for lack of eye, ear, time! The noble horse and buggy in the Prater that can tear along at a speedy clip, still leaves us the pleasure of the morning dew on the meadow, the lonely woods, the old head waters of the Danube, of pebble banks in modern faded tones of gray-brown-blue, of old pastures and cawing crow rookeries. But the speeding automobile wants to whisk away what's left of your already overly burdened soul! It wants to abduct your own sense of peace with a meanspirited spurt of speed! Roll on, destiny's children, at the tempo of a rubber-tired hack on the Praterhauptallee, cherish the riches of nature more than the pace of your passage, and above all read: Baudry de Saunier's *The Art of Driving*!

The Walking Stick

I admit it. I have a fanatic attachment to particularly striking walking sticks, it might even be the onset of an incipient mania in which one's entire lust for life is henceforth linked to lovely walking sticks. Forest, lake, spring, winter, woman, art—all fade away, and there's only one still thrilling thing left: your lovely walking stick! Even though, in my case, I do not suspect this insidious devolution of a predilection, every pet feeling in our nervous system can, alas, evolve, or realign itself into an *idée fixe*. The fact is, I know all the walking sticks for sale in Vienna, have my own special favorites in each establishment, sticks which, strange at it may seem, are the least likely to be bought by someone else. Does that surprise you, Peter Altenberg, you with your eccentric taste?! A young woman once gave me as a gift one of these passionately coveted walking sticks which stood for two years in the display case. It was made of light gray spayed goat horn and sugar cane. A remarkably successful product made in Vienna in the English style, it cost only eleven Crowns. The dear young donor sewed me a sheath of fine deer hide with brown silk for the handle.

But then they kidded in café and restaurant: "What's wrong with your Sir Stick?! Did he catch a cold in inclement weather?!?"

Somebody said: "Peter Altenberg, you're striking enough as is. Enough already with these forced efforts to make yourself ridiculous. The effect is self-evident!"

My walking stick was often knocked over. One time a man said: "Don't look so reproachful, you think I did it on purpose?!"

"No," I replied, "I don't think so; for what reason would you have to deliberately knock down my poor walking stick?!"

"There, you see, just be a little sensible," said the man and pardoned me.

As a consequence of these painful occurrences, I brought my beloved walking stick back each week to the little shop in which it had been bought and asked them to make good the damages through polishing etc., etc. The salesman always replied politely: "In two to three days! No charge for the repairs!" After a while I realized that he took me for a "walking stick nut" and never even thought of sending the stick back for repair. He always said: "That's exactly how the stick came from the 'factory'! It's as if you'd divined it!" One time I noticed a tiny nick.

"But this nick is still there," I humbly maintained.

"Yes, well, that's an innate function of the organic structure of the goat horn cell tissue itself, even our factory can't iron it out — ."

Then I thought: If they had seriously filed, grated, polished it down, there would be nothing left today of my wondrous spayed goat horn handle. How can I thank you enough for your considerate wisdom: "He's a stick-nut! Better handle with kid gloves!"

A Walk

I ran into an important politician in the Stadtpark. "Well, that's all very interesting, but everyone of you writers has a screw loose!"

"Well, for heaven's sake, that's the tool of our trade. The shoemaker has a shoemaker's bench, or else he wouldn't be able to make any shoes. We have a screw loose, or else we wouldn't be able to be any different from the others and would be unable, therefore, to communicate anything special to them that they don't already know!"

"But what about those writers with no screw loose?!"

"Writers, precisely, my dear sir, they are not!"

"For once you actually seem to hit the nail on the head. Why just the other day when I went for a walk in the woods with one of those famous 'altogether normal' ones, and he suddenly screamed on the verge of despair: 'These woods are too green for me, too green, much much too green!' it first dawned on me and I recognized that he was a real great writer!"

"On the contrary, that one, in particular, was a just a fool! Any man for whom the woods are too green is no writer, but rather a fool! He really has no screw loose. He's a perfectly normal fool!"

Psychology

For some time now I've judged people by the objects they lug around, hold dear and find attractive. These things comprise a "biographical essay" about their entire being! For instance, I am highly suspicious of men who tote around walking sticks with oxidized silver handles that represent something or other, like a dog's head, a snake or even a ravishing little curly headed damsel. Of course, these fellows can resort to the excuse that they got it as a gift from a dear friend; but first of all, no one ought not to have such tasteless friends (two negatives, alas, make a positive), and second, you can also take a friend's gift and knock him on the head with it. In any case, among cultivated people, I'm for the exchange of "coupons" in any given transaction! I'm also suspect of pink, light blue and screaming red silk, whereas satin, velvet or damask are to be counted among the "mild infractions against common decency." Printed, not woven, ties are cause for considerable concern, although the "nature-peasant pattern" is a pardonable sin. To be dressed "in a single color" from head to toe is the "latest Aristocratic craze," 1913! An open neck is highborn. High collars are nonsense, except for storks. Not to be able to make all the twists and turns of a first class acrobat from the "Apollo Theater" in any given garb is positively low class! Trousers can never be wide enough and are still far too tight! To leave the bottom button of a waistcoat open is a miserable lapse of etiquette. To anyone who claims he doesn't want to appear too conspicuous I respectfully reply that even Beethoven's Adagios were conspicuous, conspicuously beautiful! "In all things we must distinguish ourselves from the horde!" "That's what they're wearing these days—!" is dirty low-down drivel.

"Good morning, Sir, how's the world treating you?!" I said to a stranger strolling up the "Upper Semmering Pathway" in a top hat.

"Very well indeed in this lovely mountain terrain; but from where, may I ask, do you know me?"

"I know you like the back of my hand since the day you were born, as I see you've donned a top hat here—."

"I owe that to my position in the world, my good man—."

"I was immediately struck by that too, that you owe something or other to someone or other—!"

Discovery

"The 'most perfect woman' on earth came to see me today at five P.M. at the café! Miss Mitzi Thumb."

"Oh, I already discovered that number, two years before you on the Lido, Hotel Excelsior. So don't flatter yourself in that regard!"

"Discovered, discovered? How did you accomplish such a feat? Wherein did your discovery manifest itself?!"

"Manifest itself?! It manifested itself quite simply in that I saw her in her silk bathing singlet with the red patent leather belt, and was enchanted by her perfection!"

"So that's what you call discovery!? You kept it to yourself, swallowed your enchantment, deliberately made sure no one else noticed, especially not the lady on account of whom your pitifully cowardly instinct for self-preservation compels you to restrain yourself! You did nothing for this discovered perfection, just turned your head away from such splendor, which could only rock the boat of your paltry relationship! Do you know what it means to discover?!? To discover means to beat the drum for someone so that the whole world absolutely must take notice; it means to go all out for her so that everyone else grows pale, sick and poisoned with envy; to scream, cry and declaim, to disavow, demean, blot out and obliterate all others! That is: an exceptional, singular, complete discovery!"

"Peter, you're the carnival barker of life! Not everybody is so inclined. It's a profession like any other. But you have to have the nerve for it. You've got it."

"Discovery means: to make the blind see, the deaf hear, to make the callous feel, and turn the greedy into squanderers! It means: to take the gamble that this goddess you discovered turns her attention to those who without you would never have 'discovered' her. It means: to see yourself all too soon abused and abandoned, the sole mark of gratitude that the discovered one will dish out! To suffer the destiny of the discoverer, ignominious as it is, that's: discovery!"

Persecution Complex

Is it already the preliminary sign of a persecution complex if I take along on a trip twelve of my special mother-of-pearl shirt buttons, just in case? This premonition of a possible catastrophe concerning my perfectly flawless brand new shirt?! In any case, the brain that does not concern itself under such circumstances with this distressing eventuality is the healthier one, the less irritable, the less upsetable by life's little ups and downs.

The obsession with "possible unpleasantries in the coming days" is indeed a consequence of persecution complex, weakening our resilience for life. Consequently every truly discerning soul suffers from persecution complex. He is always and in every situation a profound pessimist. Only in this way does he compel himself to elude conceivable perils. He need not dwell on fortuitous events. They happen by themselves. But to smell the pitfalls in every affair, that's the important thing and that at the same time is what makes you mentally imbalanced!

"To step with the left foot on every sewer grating brings good luck, avoids bad luck. I don't really believe in it. But what does it cost me to do it?! From that moment on, you're in the snare of that unlikely trap. For if but once you fail to follow the rule, you will relentlessly trace each and every misfortune that befalls you back to that lapse. That's why you concentrate with an almost feverish frenzy to make sure to tread on every sewer grating with your left foot. But this, in turn, makes you irritable, nervous, consumed by the fear that you might, nevertheless, if but once, have missed a grating. You put yourself to the test, try intentionally to overstep a grating, and soon enough you're consumed by a curious disquiet, uncertainty; you reproach yourself, bemoan — the slightest mishap, and there you have the pernicious "logical consequence"! If only I'd stepped on the sewer grating with my left foot!

With every woman of whom you're sincerely fond you run a billion risks at every hour of losing her for whatever reason. But the man not inclined to persecution complex, that is, the idiot, the nincompoop, doesn't sense the danger, it does not enter his clear consciousness. He is blessed with the good luck, the healthy disposition to suffer an eventual catastrophe when it comes, but not the imperceptible and, therefore, all the more awful, things leading up to it. Any man not prone to a "persecution complex" in regard to a beloved never for a moment actually truly loved that person!

An old lady once said to me: "I am compelled from year to year to follow the solemn dictates of religion all the more strictly. For the closer I find myself to the final reckoning the more I fear it!"

Religion is a kind of "ideal application" of persecution complex on the human nerves!

I once said to a businessman: "You shouldn't overextend your business out into the sticks, it's financially dangerous, risky—." Whereupon he replied: "But our whole business depends on that. You've just got to have the nerves to tough it out—."

A year later he went bust. I reminded him of our conversation. Then he said to me: "You were right. But if I'd followed your advice I'd have gone bust long before!"

"My dear friend, you really ought not to leave your lovely young wife alone so long in the country—."

"You're right; but if I didn't let her go I'd lose her all the sooner—!"

Persecution complex, in any case, has one advantage, at least you can't accuse yourself of having been "a dunce." And in these tough times that's not something to sneeze at!

Perhaps the intellectual assurance of being able to avoid certain dangers in life provides a greater happiness than the heroism of leaping head-first into life and courting one's imminent demise! Heroism and persecution complex are the absolute opposites. The one heeds nothing, the other everything! The one sees victories everywhere, the other nothing but defeats. The one is a nincompoop and the other is a wise man! But can the wise man ever really be unhappy and the nincompoop ever really happy?!?

Persecution complex within reason is the capacity to foresee coming misfortune and the capacity by the force of intelligence, wherever possible, to avoid it! The opposite of that is the certainty of stupidity, that is one's so-called "quiet good fortune!"

January, on the Semmering*

January 25. The sun is trying to melt the snow. Here and there the snow fades to gray and dissolves, readying the way for spring. In Glognitz, Christmas roses poke through the snow. Everything, everything else is buried under, silent. With the steel tip of my alpenstock I trace a girl's name in the frosted glass of a shop window. Who's name?! What do you care?! My soul is suffering. For four days now I've sheltered a little lady bug. It lives on the condensation under a glass. It even spreads its wings. I'll buy it a bouquet of mimosa, yellow, sweet-scented blossoms with little gray-green leaves. How did it manage to weather the winter until now, to live through all of winter's perils? I don't know. The temperature already hit 18 degrees Celsius, without its protector P.A.?! How did I myself manage to endure it all?! I don't know. I write a girl's name in the frosted glass of a shop window on the main drag. Who's name?! What do you care?! My soul is suffering, so it's still alive, it's still alive! The little lady-bug under the glass thinks: "Ha, ha, ha, it's warm here but there's not much to eat; we'll just have to wait it out till February; we're bound to find something then — ." Little creatures always find what they need.

---

*A popular mountain resort in Austria

The Steamboat Landing

I love the steamboat landings on the Salzkammergut Lakes, the old gray-black ones and the newer yellow ones. They smell so good, as if from years of soaked-up baking in the sun. In the water round their thick pylons scores of minuscule gray-silver fish are forever scuttling here and there, suddenly swarming in one place, suddenly dispersing and disappearing. The water smells so delightful under these landing docks, like the skin of fresh fish. When a steamboat docks, all the pylons rise and the landing gathers all its strength to endure the shock. The steamboat engine with its red paddle-wheels fights a stubborn battle with the obstinate landing holding it off. The landing will not yield, defending itself, so it seems, only insofar as it is absolutely necessary, while trembling with the force of its inner resolve. At last its quiet perseverance wins out and the boat lets loose, gives way, sails off again.

For hours and hours the landing lies in wait for steamboats, withering in the heat of the sun, lonesome, shunned.

All of a sudden agitated people in light clothing approach and amass themselves on the landing. "Don't step too far forward," the parents warn and look at the landing as an imminent danger. I could well observe with some justification: "Somewhere, apart from the rest, two figures silently lean body to body against the railing." But that's an observation of the old school and so it's best to keep it to oneself. Still I can't deny that an obstinate stare of extended duration down into the depths from the railing, while standing in the close proximity of a young lady, often elicits its own loud and clear, albeit unspoken, response. On the landing boards, fish too small to eat are sacrificed. You catch them, hurl them against the wood, gloating over their dance of death. It's true that between the teeth of a little pike dying is hardly a pleasant spectacle. But who after all ever dies peacefully in bed. Sometimes the landings are also crowded with the committees and the presidiums of yacht races. Sailboat regattas. For hours on end they peer through binoculars at a mysterious spot in the lake, and nobody else has the vaguest idea what's going on. Still, everyone's excited.

Here and there a technical remark is overheard. Suddenly the crowd cries hurrah and notes are frantically scribbled. Now the landing is like the hilltop perch of a field marshal surveying a battle. Everyone follows the outcome with his binoculars. And the landing lies right there in the thick of things. But then again, on moonlit nights it lies like a dark leviathan, reaching forth, stretching its blackness out over the silver lake.

I love the steamboat landings on the Salzkammergut Lakes, the old gray-black ones and the newer yellow ones. They are for me a sort of sign of summer freedom, summer serenity, scented as if from years of soaked-up baking in the sun.

In Munich

For several days now I've been in Munich for the very first time. I haven't seen a thing yet, not a thing listed in the little guidebooks, no monuments, no paintings. I'm not interested in the things that were. I'm interested in the things that are, that will be! Look! The new art is beaming out at me from the show windows of the fine stores, the stuff that would transform the lot of us shriveling in life's stranglehold into visionary artist-folk if only we could spend hours and hours gazing at it, each in our own cubicle back home. Europeans, where are you stuck in the mud?!? Joylessly you still display your Meissen figurines and vases in your hand-carved cabinets! You're deceiving yourselves!

You live without any real affinity for the wondrous colors and forms of nature itself, say "ah!" to odd and unappealing things, feed off catch phrases and history, buy vases with blossoms that never bloomed! You've got eyes that can't savor what they see in and of itself, but are, rather, swayed by names and pre-set patterns! Which is why, since you take no advantage of these most precious organs, you fail to plunder the treasures of these two inexhaustibly rich eyes, you remain miserable, empty, sad, try to soak up the pleasures of other organs, fleeting pleasures gone in a flash! Then come the long gaping hours, time that needs to be killed with the poisons "drinking," "gambling—!"

But look, the new, the modern artist wants to reunite you with nature and its profound splendors! He wants to gently open your eyes to the gleam of life itself, not to the lure of false phantasy figures that have lost their effect! You really ought to hear the gurgle of hidden springs, not the crash of cascades! Your eyes ought to be joined in loving wedlock to the things of this world, celebrate a solemn union, a noble bond!

But you hold back, make do with rubbish! See how close the little boy is to nature when he sneaks up on the wondrous Apollo butterfly perched on the mountain thistle?! Or the little girl weaving a wreath of wildflowers?! Life comes later, makes them blind, empty! Then they play lawn-tennis on the meadow in nature! Lawn-tennis, I tell you! Hot cheeks with cold souls!

Learn from the Japanese! When the cherry trees blossom, the people flock to look, stand silently for hours on end before the white-rose splendor. No benches and tables are set up for gorging and swilling. This artistic people stand in silence before the white-rose splendor, for hours on end! Back in their rooms, on immaculate, noble, delicate yellow-brown partitions hang bamboo baskets with fine flowers. Both men and women stop by, look at the baskets of flowers and leave again, returning in silence to the tasks of the day.

But what sort of gewgaws do you have crowding your desktops and your walls?! You have them and that's it! What's there to look at?! You own them but you don't love them!

Better to display the true artworks of nature under glass, wonderful exotic bugs or noble mussels in flat hues! These shades of bugs, mussels, butterflies, stones, the true shapes of blossoms and leaves embody the "new artists" for you in the applied arts. Put their work in show windows. They make a gift to you of nature in all her glory, nature which no one ever grows tired of admiring— no one who ever really truly looked with those eyes that are the direct link to the soul and the spirit, those eyes that have become the seeing spirit, the observant soul itself!

What kind of junk are you amassing?! Shame on you! Possession!? Dear God, possession must be something like the possession of one's skin, one's hands! It belongs to you, is indispensable, envelops, so to speak, your entire being, and is an essential part of the same, your most external self, above and beyond your epidermis. That which stands on my table top and hangs on my walls belongs to me, like my skin and my hair. It lives with me, in me, off me. Without it I'd virtually be a vestigial, stunted wastrel. Take, for instance, my lady friend, the "lady with the golden curls," and the painting by Burne-Jones: "A girl sits reclining in a garden by the seashore, her hands resting on an old book in her lap. Two angels are fiddling for the reclining girl who has her hands folded on the old book, dreaming in that garden by the seashore; they're hovering above book and garden, carrying her away, but whereto, whereto?!" This painting and the "departed lady," above whose bed it hung, were one! Whoever grasped the painting grasped her, whoever grasped her grasped the painting. No other tableau could have hung above her bed. It belonged to her, to her, like her hands and hair. The lady lends an ear, but whereto, whereto?!

People of the future, you must surround yourselves with such things that truly belong to you, are one with you! The new artist fashions such things out of his genius, works conceived for your souls! Things that really belong to you! Just paint your walls white and set in a corner or hang on the wall one of those wondrous cups glazed with the hue of the hummingbird, the setting sun and the white of breaking waves!

I saw a light brown vase here with highlights of gold and dark stripes that dampened the effect. And another yellowish one with milky white hue that made it look pale. And yet another luminous one in the shape of a giant beehive with cells glazed a waxy yellow. And one like the ephemeral green wings of May flies. And still another dark blue vase, its blueness fading to the color of the early morning sky, night breaking into day, and then darkening again, the color of night. Then there were light brown spherical glass bulbs on glass bamboo stalks, a lovely composition. Gallé glasses; light brown flowers appear to emerge foglike out of the glass itself, and yet do not emerge, disappearing in the swirl.

Such vases would not stand forsaken in your cubicles back home! Such vases elicit a gentle love! When you walk into the room you salute them. And when you leave you salute them again. Intimate companions!

So paint your walls white, keep the decor as simple as possible, put up things you can love, like brothers, sisters of the soul, not cold dohickeys, strangers! Then you'll be rich and never lonesome! For several days now I've been in Munich for the very first time. I haven't seen a thing yet, not a thing listed in the little guidebooks, no monuments, no paintings. I'm not interested in the things that were. I'm interested in the things that are, that will be! But the "new art" beamed out at me from the show windows of the fine stores as I ambled alone down the lovely streets.

My Summer Trip, 1916

Three box cars heaped with hay were burning on an endlessly long freight train carting hay between Rekawinkel and Neulengbach. We had to wait somewhere for an hour and a half. So I was obliged to stop over in Amstetten* from eleven in the morning til four in the afternoon.

I saw meadows that no man had ever tread. I heard birds in the beechwood forest or squirrels cracking beechnuts and letting the shells fall. I saw a girl of thirteen years standing in front of the work house with unbelievably lovely long and slender feet and toes, barefoot, of course. She sensed how I worshiped her naked feet. She followed me for a good long stretch, stopped, then gave up. I will never forget her. And one day she will say to her lover or bridegroom: "You'll never be able to look me deep in the eyes and see all the way down to where our better self lives, like that old nut did that day, August 5, 1916, at two in the afternoon!" Three boxcars heaped with hay were burning directly in front of us and all the other passengers were up in arms, all except for a young lieutenant who was missing a right leg but made do with a pair of elegant, feather-light yellow bamboo crutches, who said: "Dear ladies, it's generally a good deal more dreary in the trenches than it is here in Amstetten!"

---

*Amstetten, a town in Lower Austria on the Ybbs River

My Gmunden

You're already making a long face reading this title.

Aha, yet another depiction in his matchless condensed manner of "seashores," "evening atmospheres," "water's eternal newness," we know all that. No, this time something else! In autumn I was once the last guest left of the summer season. One evening, a middle-aged baron and learned doctor of philosophy introduced himself, his family was native to these parts. He requested the honor of my acquaintance. Of course! He was very cultivated and very well bred. On the eighth day of our incipient acquaintance he said to me one evening in the course of a stroll:

"Why, pray tell, don't you give up your criminal plans to take my life?!"

"Since I have no such plans, I cannot give them up!"

"I have nothing against you personally, you are merely the operative agent of a higher power to whom both you and I are beholden! Nevertheless, exceptionally, I enjoin you to cease and desist in this plot to bring about my annihilation, socially, and in all other senses!" From then on I let myself be drawn into this peculiar duel between a healthy spirit (my own) and a sick one in the naïve hope of making him realize through logical argument the folly of his delusion. Unfortunately, each acknowledgment that he'd been wrong about me made him all the more unhappy, desperate and, above all, dogged in his resolve! In his view, I was simply being shrewder, more cunning in my deception. For instance, he bought himself ten Egyptian cigarettes. Upon his emergence from the tobacconist's, he said: "The cigarettes were poisoned on your orders!" I suggested he save them for me, said I'd smoke them all in front of his eyes from then till nightfall. Whereupon he hissed: "Swindler!"

One evening he said: "I hope your supper tastes particularly good this evening!" "Why?" "Because it's your last!" Whereupon he pulled out a Browning revolver. He walked me home as usual. I switched on the light in my room, after ten minutes switched it off again, remained seated in the dark for a half hour, then I ventured down the street to see the mayor, Dr. Wolfsgruber. The old man lay sick in bed. Upon learning the name of the person in question the mayor passed word through his chambermaid: He'd receive me in his downstairs parlor, but without any lights on. He said to me: "You have my profound thanks on behalf of our little town! Don't go to bed, take the earliest train out, unfortunately we thought he was harmless! Thanks again, and be assured of my prompt attention to all necessary actions that must, alas, be taken, in light of your report!"

It was, however, the opinion of the dear little town that "meshuganeh attract each other!"

An Experience

Hans Schliessmann implored me to come out Friday night to the Park Hotel in Hietzing, where the spirited and tasteful Dostal, band member of the 26ers, was concertizing solo in the large and lovely garden. The concert ended at twelve midnight and Schliessmann was concerned I should catch the last tram home. But it rattled right past us. At that very moment an elegant rubber-tired coach pulled up directly in front of us, and two sassy girls' voices cried out with joy: "Peter, Jesus, Peter, what ever are you doing here in Hietzing?!" — "I missed the last tram," I replied, business-like, and without any overt exuberance at the pleasure of seeing the lovely, racy girls again. — "Don't you worry now, Peter, we'll take you along in our carriage, we're headed for Vienna anyways, what a lucky coincidence — ." Hans Schliessmann stood there greatly stirred in the face of such a true rare stroke of luck, thanked the kind, eye-catching, dainty darlings on behalf of his enviable friend and said that the "golden Viennese heart" was, after all, not yet altogether on the verge of extinction, as he had previously conjectured — .

We drove off. At Mariahilferberg, one of the sweet young things said: "Say Peter, how much're you gonna pay the cabby?!" — To which I replied: "Nothing. I was invited." — "Well for Chrissake, you cheapskate, it's just a measly Crown or two." For the payee it's always "costly Crowns," for the recipient it's only "a measly Crown or two." I replied: "I'm your guest." — "Don't tell me you was gonna drag your bones all the way to Vienna on foot, you fruitcake?!" — "If push came to shove, I might've hailed a hansom." — "There you are, so you see, it comes down to the same." — "In that case, I'll contribute what the hansom would've cost — ." — "Will ya get a load o' that, the guy rides in a rubber-tired coach and wants to pay the price of a hansom, well I'll be damned — ." — "Alright, so how much do I owe?!" — "Ten Crowns, that's pennies." — I did not feel that it was pennies, but I inquired: "Why ten Crowns, if I may ask?!" — "So what if we already drove around a little in Hietzing on such a lovely evening before picking you up, you tightwad, would you grudge us the pleasure!?"—I replied that I would gladly grant them that."—"So, you see, you're a gentleman, after all, you're our good Peter, ain't ya—." So their good Peter shelled out the ten Crowns. "What about us, don't we deserve a little something?!" said the two sweet things. "Ain't our company worth something to ya, or are we just appetizers before the main course, for Chrissake —?" I gave each of them another Crown. "Peter, Peter, we always took ya for a true poet, a better sort, an idealistically inclined kind o' guy; don't tell me we was wrong—." I called for the coach to stop, got out. "You ain't sore, are you, Peter?!"—"No. Why should I be sore?!" "—So didn't you find the ride amusing?!"—"Very," I replied. That very night I wrote Hans Schliessmann a card: "Concerning your correction of a prior conjecture concerning the demise of the 'golden Viennese heart,' I bid you hold off on that correction until next Friday when Dostal of the 26ers once again concertizes at the Park Hotel, Hietzing. More to follow straight from the horse's mouth—."

The next day I ran into one of the sweet young things. "Peter, lucky I should run into you. Right after you got out yesterday, I got to climb up onto the coach box and drive the rig, and Mr. coach-man, he climbed in with Mitzl in the passenger compartment and pulled the shades. And then he went and gave us your ten Crowns. There's a proper gentleman, let that be a lesson to you!" I hastened to write to Hans Schliessmann: "Your first inclination was correct. The 'golden Viennese heart' is still alive and well."

In a Viennese *Puff* *

"Say," said the sweet, cuddly one to me, "that guy over there ain't normal; he lives on a sandy island in the Danube, runs around half-naked, will ya get a load of him, he's brown all over from the sun. He only comes here to sneer at us! At you too, Peter, you too. What's the use of all your pretty poetry?"

The fellah over there really did look like life itself. Or like an African traveler. His hide tanned tough by light and air, tanned I tell you.

His friends at his table had all "fallen in love," technically speaking.

So now they all nudged him to likewise finally "fall in love."

"You want me to go weak?" the brown one replied to the pale faces. And everyone laughed.

"Some strength you got in you if you ain't got none to spend!?" said sweet Anna.

"Let 'im be —," said Hansi, "everybody knows what he's gotta do. Even the sun probably don't do him no good no more —."

"Do you despise me too?" said the tanned man, turning to one of the girls who was reading a dime novel, totally immersed in it.

"Why should I despise you? I don't even know you."

"How did you get started in this kind of life?" said the natural man softly. Such is the standard question of all dilettantes of life.

"My story wouldn't interest the gentleman much —."

"On the contrary. You seem to me to have been born for something better!" Second standard line of the dilettante!

"I was corrupted —."

"Aha, by love!"

"No, not love!"

"Then by desire!"

"No, they plied me with drink, on a picnic —."

"By alcohol then! It's got to have been one of the three poisons —."

---

*Viennese slang for brothel

He categorized it all under the rubric "alcohol."

Anna brushed by and said: "Hey, Mr. Robinson Crusoe, don't you go and corrupt this innocent thing—."

The Danube island man walked over to the open window, peered out at the darkness of the narrow street lit only with a glaring fleck of light from the pissoir, and took in a breath of the foul air with evident disgust. Then he said: "You've got too little respect for sunlight and fresh air, that's your problem!"

The girls were momentarily befuddled by the thought that they actually might perhaps have too little respect for sunlight and fresh air. Since up till then they really had no respect for it at all.

Only Friederike, who never wanted to hear her named shortened into "Fritzerl" because she was the one they always called that, spoke up: "Well, we've got a better sense of humor than you, Mister—."

"Zip it," said the other girls, "don't hurt the guy's feelings, that ain't right—."

"Farewell, you fallen soul!" said the man and left.

"With our best regards, Mr. Robinson Crusoe—," Anna called after him.

"What'd you all tell me to zip it for when I put that sorry sap in his place?!?" said Friederike.

"You can't just go 'n rub their nose in the truth; he might still have picked one to take upstairs—."

"No way, not that sun nut; all his sun-soaked strength makes him weak where it counts—."

Putain

The little room is flooded with the scent of a mountain meadow. In the light brown wash basin lies a thick bunch of Daphne Cneorum, rose-colored asters.

"Daphne Cneorum —," he remarks upon entering, savoring all the types of alpine laurel with their fine fragrance and color, and thinks of mountainsides bathed in sunlight.

"The hell with my flowers —," she says. "What do you care what they're called —?"

She undresses and crawls into bed.

"Say, what'd Max mean?! Are you fellahs really not going to come by no more?"

"No —," he says, "it costs money and people talk. What are we, whoremongers?! For heaven's sake!"

Silence.

"Well then, that's that —," she says softly.

He inhales the clear scent of woman's breath and mountain meadow.

She lies there motionless.

Then she says: "It's a damn shame, it is —. I was proud of you all, proud —. I always said: 'My friends —!' Maybe I didn't act like I should have. I shoulda pulled the wool over your eyes, made a scene, a comedy —."

"Come on, sweetheart, don't be such a child —," he says and kisses her hand.

"You're fine fellahs, ain't you —," she says, "fine as silk! Why'd you bother coming?! What for?! Nothing to be done —. That's all: 'Nothing to be done about it.' I can't put it into pretty words, but that's all —. I got thoughts in my head too, see —. That Robert, he's such a dear. I'll tell you a little story. But you can't go blabbing it around town. One time he said to me: "You're tired, Anna, better sleep —." " 'S'at what we came up for?!" I says. "Tired is tired —," he says. "It's just like after a hike in the mountains —." Ain't that sweet, though —?! I really did fall asleep. Why did I trust him? He's not really my type. But he said: "Go ahead, Anna, sleep!"

Silence. She sighs. Silence—.

"You're a fine lot. Fine as silk. I'm really gonna miss you's—."

Silence.

"Nothing to be done—. Tell Max—."

"Tell him what?!"

"Nothing———."

Silence.

"Why'd you ever bother coming?! What for?! I don't get it. You're fine as silk. I think I'm gonna dry up—."

The little room smells of Daphne Cneorum—.

She climbs out of bed and plunks herself in an easy chair.

Then she opens the Venetian blinds and the morning spills in like a mountain stream.

"Shut the blind—," he says.

She lets down the blind, crawls back into bed.

"I have friends, three friends—!! Black Bertha, she'll never get it. The dumbbell! Listen up—my heart is hurting."

He says: "Alright then, we'll be back. But what good does it do you?! We just bother you. Anyways, come June, we're going away. Max is going to the seashore, Robert's going to the mountains———."

She: "Am I holding you back or what———?!"

She falls asleep.

He feels inside: "Sleep! Extinguisher of consciousness, wave breaker—!"

He thinks: "We're like dumb fate, breaking and entering a human heart, tearing open the white gates of friendship, letting the light come spilling in like a mountain stream—! Then we go and say: 'What are we, whoremongers?! For heaven's sake, sweetheart, give us a break—!' 'Adieu,' she says softly. 'Am I holding you back or what—?!' That's just the way life is, we tell ourselves. A splendid excuse!"

The little room is flooded with the scent of Daphne Cneorum. It's like the incense of mountain meadows—.

The poor soul sleeps.

Sleep-extinguisher of consciousness! Wave breaker—!

Human Relations

The two well-established artists sat together in a little after-hours café engaged in a heated discussion on the innate brutality evident in the "I-ism" of one's fellow man! They stressed the term "*I*-ism" as if thereby precisely to emphasize the fact that: The rest of the world says "Egotism!"

Whereupon the young lady seated nearby said: "What the hell are you two talking about, huh?! What's all this crap supposed to mean? Listen up, just this morning my madame herself served me with a signed writ of seizure. That don't exist, does it, a personally signed and delivered writ of seizure?! It don't exist! Right?"

"Pardon, Miss, but we're no lawyers—."

"Who needs lawyers?! Listen up! Anybody with a little book learning has got to know that there ain't never been no such thing as a personally signed and delivered writ of seizure! Can you imagine such a thing!? The whole world would be doing nothing else but serving each other writs! Just use your brains a little, fellahs, will ya?!"

The artists discussed the fact that the puffed-up Mr. B. is so full of himself that he hears and sees nothing, like a woodcock in a fir tree. Can't always keep claiming to be blinded by sexual frenzy like the wild fowl!

The girl started whimpering about how she'd been personally served with a signed writ of seizure by her madame. She once again explained to the gentlemen that there ain't never been no such thing as a personally signed and delivered writ of seizure.

So the gentlemen agreed that they'd never heard of such a thing and started kissing up to the girl, presuming her to be somewhat consoled now that they'd concurred.

But the young lady wasn't quite yet up to it. So the gentlemen told her that she'd missed her calling in life; that she was a weepy whore. If she went on like that she'd never lure a lousy dog.

The girl just stared at the end of her nose: "There ain't no such thing as a personally signed and delivered writ of seizure!"

Now the artists took a somewhat more participatory stance and said: "How much do you actually owe her? How much can it possibly be?!"

The girl replied hopefully: "35 Guldens!"

The artists: "What?! For such a pittance?! And that's all she's blubbering about! Well for crying out loud, you can easily pay it off in installments!"

The girl felt: "Deadbeats, go hang yourselves!"

The artists went ahead and figured out that in weekly installments of only five Guldens she could pay it all off in less than seven weeks. Every penny of it. Or else she could pay it off in monthly installments of 20 Guldens. Or, better yet, daily, a Gulden a day. They agreed that a Gulden a day would be best.

The girl sat there and kept on crying.

The artists got fed up and left.

Outside they said: "What's the use of trying to help a body? You go figure your head off for a stranger! And what do you get for your troubles?! Ingratitude!"

Now the down at the heels waiter walked up to the girl: "Listen, honey, what do you say the two of us head to the courthouse together at 8 A.M.!? There ain't never been no such thing as a personally signed and delivered writ of seizure! This country's got laws!"

So they went home together to hammer out the details. There were another three hours left till 8 A.M., which time they put to good use.

At 8 A.M., her prince in shining armor said to her: "Know what, Mitzi, it's better not to start any trouble with a court of law. I'm sure your madame ain't that mean-hearted. Know what, Mitzi, better pay it back in installments!"

By this time, the girl was all wiped out, and muttered softly as she dozed off: "There ain't never been no such thing as a personally signed and delivered writ of seizure. Ain't that right, Bud?!"

The New Romanticism

Heinrich Frauenlob, Walter von der Vogelweide, Hölty, Hölderlin, where are you tonight?!? Are your velvet doublets moth-eaten, are your locks all tousled by the storm?!

Here I stand, a seventeen-year-old, in the dead of night on the veranda of a country villa, with my nightgown open, ready to drop my comb so that you can press it against your lips and carry it around down darkened streets, your lips infused with silent songs.

Where are you?!? You dreamy ones?! Dreamers dreaming of us!?

Gentlemen, I danced this afternoon on the lawn in the melancholic old Herzogspark, held my dress with both hands and danced—.

Will you please dream of it tonight, dream of me dancing in the melancholic old Herzogspark holding my dress in both my hands??

Will nobody dream of it tonight?!?

Dream, will you please dream of it! You dreamless ones!

Listen up, gentlemen! I danced this afternoon on the lawn in the melancholic old Herzogspark naked as the day I was born; and I held no dress in my two hands, for I had none on and was naked!

Dream of it! You dreamless ones!

Oh you wretch, you wretch! You took me and used me—!

But dream of it! Dream of it, I beg you, at least this night and the next!

No, he did not dream of it, but slept soundly and deeply like a satiated beast—.

Cabaret Fledermaus

The Cabaret Fledermaus really goes all out to please. Following the appearance of the universally acclaimed and much heralded Wiesenthal Sisters, the Cabaret now brings us a young Moroccan dancer. And all this at a time of day, five in the afternoon, when "the idle world" is particularly prone to idling around. Well now you can wile away the time with the exceptional. The altogether new is preferable to the habitual, as pithy as the latter may be. It's an energizing stimulant like tea, coffee, cigarettes. However skeptical and reserved you might be, something or other of the inertly traditional is rattled and disturbed. You start tallying up your carefully guarded capital of what was, sifting out the true worth; it spawns a change in you, a change for the better. For the stamp collector who suddenly sees that coins are also beautiful, it's the beginning of a recognition that both may be beside the point, not an end to which to devote your life! But something must move forward in us, move forward, forward march! Morocco introduces a new rhythm in our limbs. Long live Morocco! We see before us an unaccustomed kind of light brown skin, muscles developed in an unaccustomed way. The sword dance is strangely astonishing, the belly dance is strangely stirring. How wondrous is woman's body without the deception of drapery! It is so natural that one can no longer fathom that crime "tricot." Goethe once admired for hours on end a young woman in her God-given perfection. He was happy not to touch even her fingertips. He considered himself sufficiently satisfied at the mere sight of her. He went away pleased as never before. Our sense of modesty focuses on imperfection. It gets caught up with that which is hidden, rightfully indignant that what we see does not bespeak the original concept of the Creator. But the orange-colored skin of Sulamit Rahu passes the test of perfection before the eye of the artist. The nobly grotesque dance of Gertrude Barrison in her green costume designed by Kolo Moser, in which she resembles a new unknown species of bird, carries us away to likewise exceptional worlds. In one of the dancer's indescribably lovely and engaging spoken texts she declares before starting to dance that all women conform in a cowardly fashion to that to which they are spiritually or economically beholden. Beholden only to her own spirit, she, however, sought to ensnare no one, not even the public. What follows then is a grotesque dance infused with the friskiness and clowning of a child. On top of all that a hairdo that ought to catch on among others endowed with an equally lovable face! But only among them! The third exceptional act is Lina Loos. An uncommon personality, she delivers her extraordinary recitation accompanied by an oboe and in blue moonlight. The young lady expresses her pain and her despair that the man in question does not respond romantically. She dreams of Minnesänger* and an entanglement with Mr. So and So. A veritable Altenberg in a newfangled frame. We see before us a wonderfully attractive and frustrated woman, whose complaint we fathom directly, not merely through the byway of a sympathetic poet's heart. And that oboe melody is so poetic! Band leader Scherber composed it. The whole thing is presented as an attack on the feeble reality of daily life. That's why everyone is initially against it and almost offended by it. Even for carefree kids there's only one Christmas a year, one birthday, one nameday. And with grownups, isn't it all the more so? The holidays of the soul and the senses are all too scarce. Poets keep proclaiming them but they never come! So we resign ourselves and make do with the puff. What else can we do? In any case, we'd better not scorn the dreaming poets who point the way to that which we might actually need!

---

*German troubadours

Newsky Roussotine Troop

How miserable you feel on summer evenings in the big city. As if you've been left behind. Bypassed. For instance, I go walking after dark on the Praterstrasse! It's as if I and those I pass had flunked life's final exam and—, while the good pupils were permitted to enjoy their vacation by way of recompense. But we are only allowed to dream.

"Oh waves crashing against old wooden docks; oh little lonesome lake; oh clearings sparsely grown with grass and brown bog, where every private tutor will tell you: "You see? This is where deer come in the evening to drink." Oh elder brush with black musk beetles and little metallic-looking mountain beetles and louse-ridden rose beetles and light brown mountain flies beside babbling brooks slipping over big stones at a speedy clip! And the brush nourishes insect worlds! Oh 22-degree well bubbling forth in an open basin on which linden blossoms float; for the pathway to the swimming hole is bordered with linden trees, and everything is covered with linden blossoms! White sailboat serenity in lacquered yachts! The ladies lightly tanned. The whole world trimming down. Who's going to win the regatta?! Risa, give me your hand on the pier. Noontimes loaded with 10,000 tons of solar heat, like the weight of war ships; afternoons with apricots, sour cherries, noble gooseberries; evenings with chilled Giesshübler;* at night—do you hear the swans opening and closing their beaks?! And again, the swans opening and closing their beaks?! And nothing more—."

But we wander down the Praterstrasse in the big city. 8 P.M. Akin to all the failing shops on either side. Peaches in bins beside matjes herrings. Baskets full of this and that. Bathing caps. Black radishes. Bicycle lights blinking everywhere. As if the air, like in perfume factories bursting with the scent of violets, had here soaked itself full of the smells of potato salad, tar sandwiched between granite pavement slabs and millefleur de l'homme épuisé!

---

*A wine punch

Arc lights burning as feebly as glow worms on summer nights could hardly make matters any worse. Summer misery all lit up! Leave it in the dark, if you please, to lower in silent shadows! But arc lights scream: "Take a look!" They screech out life's lapses, spilling the beans in their white light!

"Venice in Vienna," 11:30 P.M.: Performance of the Newsky Roussotine Troop. Just a hop, skip and a jump away from the Praterstrasse and summer's illuminated misery. As if you were to wake up on the Semmering after having fallen asleep in an air thick with red brick dust! Newsky Roussotine Troop. They dance like noble princesses!

Every movement sings out. "You heap of crippled, crawling, downtrodden slaves, see us swing free! We come from the Russian folk soul! We're poems straight from the steppes!"

As if far removed from life's insufficiencies, they peer at you, standing there with inordinately noble faces and red flowers in their hair; long, pale green strands of pearls hang down the front of their white silken gowns.

The songs, the dances are Russia incarnate. That's how you learn to recognize Russia. It's like a journey into the heart of the Czarist empire. No books can convey it. Or perhaps you'd rather read about the "noble melancholy" of the people who live there, about "the freedom ringing in their souls," about the forests of birch trees and the embroidery in red and green?!?

Better, you mere mortal, keep your eyes on the Newsky Roussotine Troop!

Behold! They sing both chorales and wails! Just as in a warm bath an infant wails and in cold life a wise man mutters: "So be it!"

Behold, the youngest member of the troop, the most Russian of Russian Misses, shakes herself from her shoulders to her toes and lets spill a wail out of this life-filled organism, a long, childlike wail — the trill of nature! And then again somebody else declaims, as it were: "Respice finem" and "requiescat" and "Moskwá, Moskwá."

And a noble lad dances his burning passion.

And the leader Newsky sings in a soft and tempered voice his clear notes, looks over with calm and assurance at the little kneeling woman, circles round, beating on a tambourine in measured tact the rhythm of life lived to the fullest.

And the noble princess, the light blond? She's the very incarnation of nature itself in all its unspeakable inexhaustible bounty. Like waving, blustering corn fields in the evening wind, like brooding black Scotch pines on lofty heights, like Beethoven's adagios, telling it all in mild notes of dejection, all the while soaring with her lofty soul over the morass of miseries—!

Here she stands and sings, the loveliest, the lightest, the blondest, woman incarnate! Model woman! Crying, as it were: "Come to me, Lord of Life!" and crying: "Keep away!" Crying: "I love you!" and crying: "I cannot love you!" Crying: "Take me as a simple creature," and crying: "Take me as the hundredfold soul of the world all!" Crying: "Take me in your arms, all-merciful man!" and crying: "Nay! Kiss me only from afar with your soft winks!" Crying: "Make me your servant!" and crying: "Make me your master!" Crying: "Can you be like that, oh Man, that I bind myself to you, to your dark wilted blossom on the tree of life, your man's heart, I the wellspring, the lightest, blondest source of all."

Here she stands and calls and asks.

Bunches of red flowers bedeck her hair; pale green pearls dangle down her white silken gown.

Then suddenly the whole troop turn simple, leave Russia's steppes behind, embrace each other, bow their heads in friendship, and sing the song of life: "We will abide, we will survive!"

Late at night they all take their supper, in simple attire and sheer exhaustion, in the hidden cellar of the Johannis-Bräu, listening, amazed by the "Viennese ditties" that hover around them, that prime the soul like a horn-book for Spinoza, like the fairy tale of Little Red Riding Hood, like "Hans, who Squandered his Good Fortune" and "Of the Violet Blooming in Hiding" and "Ring Around the Rosy, a Pocket Full of Posy." Austria, what a naïve place you are! As if some poor soul unlucky in love cut himself a pipe out of reeds and merrily set to imitating bird calls!

But Newsky Roussotine Troop, whereto do you lead us?! From the miserable big city summer of the Praterstrasse to the fields of tyranny, to the realms of future strength and freedom!

It's a long way from the "common concertina" to "Newsky Roussotine." As far as from Marlitt* to Tolstoy.

It's like a battle, the evolution of the new soul of man. Everyone resists it. Many fall beforehand, in exhaustion, before the unexpected. Many fall in the rain of enemy fire. Few manage to storm the newly conquered land, planting their flags in the soil of new concepts —.

How does it fit here?! I don't know. Because I love Russia's songs?!

At 11 p.m. I wander down the Praterstrasse en route to the production of the Newsky Troop. The women wear thick bushels of red flowers in their hair, and long, pale green strands of pearls dangling down their white silken gowns. They all embrace each other and weep. They all embrace each other and wail. The noble lad dances his burning passion. Newsky, the man, beats on a tambourine in measured tact the rhythm of life lived to the fullest. Down the Praterstrasse I wander at 11 p.m.

---

*Eugenie John Marlitt (1825–1887), popular German opera singer and author

The Interpretation

I wrote in the paper concerning the dear little dancer Hedi Weingartner, that she represents in body and soul the very incarnation of the Viennese belle. My conclusion read: "And nevertheless, for all the apparent gaiety, she's so very sad inside! About what? Just ask Franz Schubert and Hugo Wolf!"

My young room service waiter said to me: "Jesus, that was swell, what you wrote about that Viennese honey. And the story with that Mr. Wolf and the other guy!"

"What do you mean?" I asked.

"You know, the two dudes that dumped that poor thing!"

"No, those are two long-dead, illustrious Viennese composers of Lieder who were cheerful on the surface and yet so very sad in their songs!"

"Aha — so that's what it's supposed to mean! To be perfectly honest, Mr. von Altenberg, I prefer my interpretation!"

Subjectivity

She said: "Ever since they demolished my dear old 'Bösendorfer Hall' (a concert hall in Vienna), I've been an unhappy person. I grant you that there are more pressing problems and tragedies in this World War, but for me, the most wretched soul alive, there are, alas — or thank God! — no others. So many heroes fall and I mourn my 'Bösendorfer Hall.' Should I, therefore, be ashamed to admit it? It was my all. When I sat there I forgot the world. I forgot the present, the future. Later, at the dinner table, I had no idea what I ate. That will never happen again. I know the other concert halls. But I don't forget the present in them or the future. Am I 'musical'!? Who knows! In the Bösendorfer Hall I was. Must one, can one possibly be it everywhere?! They're definitely 'geniuses,' the ones that can be musical everywhere. People like me are terribly attached to just one place. In that one place he revives his spirit, there he thrives, there he comes to be himself! No, more than himself. For my sake alone they couldn't very well leave the building standing, that's clear. Just once I lost my cool. Someone said to me: 'Its acoustics weren't even particularly good!' And I thought to myself: 'If I were a tigress, I'd leap at him and tear out his throat with my claws!' But unfortunately, I'm no tigress."

Aphorisms

Coquetry is the immense decency of a desirable woman, thereby, for the moment at least, to hold off the disappointments she is bound to bring you.

Man stretches woman's soul on the Procrustes bed of his own cravings.

There are three idealists: God, mothers and poets! They don't seek the ideal in completed things — they find it in the incomplete.

The People Don't Always
Feel Altogether Social-democratic

"Say, coachman, do you know a Tschecherl* still open at this hour?!?"

"I do indeed, Sir, but the clientele's too low class in that joint."

"Listen, my good man, for me there are no lower class people and no upper class people, you understand?! Everybody's equal!"

"Oh they're equal alright, but the body odor's different!"

Green grocer: "But we also have fruit for the very fancy folk?!?"

"What kind of people are they, the very fancy folk?!?"

"The very fancy folk are them that buy the very fancy fruit!"

---

*A little café

Big Prater* Swing

These are your absinthe-ecstasies of life, you girls of the people! Everything gets turned and tumbled topsy-turvy! And on the downwards swing you shriek with terror and excitement! Here you forget that the rent is overdue and that at any moment you could get knocked up and be abandoned! Here you experience your cruise-ship emotions, seasickness for 10 Kreuzer!

And later in the meadows, in the dark distant meadows!

Whistle, fellah, if you spot a cop!

---

*Vienna's famous amusement park

Sunset in the Prater

They sat for hours in the Grabenkiosk* on the last day of August, watched *fiakers*† roll by with foreigners in the passenger seats, automobiles like migrating birds returning from distant trips, ladies on the *trottoir* gliding by with astonishing self-assurance and others that pattered and pranced about to puff themselves up into something special.

At the Kiosk sat a French woman whom one dared greet only with one's eyes. And a sweet young thing with her "aunt," whom one likewise saluted with the eyes alone. And unfamiliar damsels with veiled hats whom one did not greet at all. And a few men who'd already returned from their vacations. All these people felt a little déclassé to have been spotted at the Grabenkiosk in the high season, while the others were still basking in Ostende or Biarritz — .

Notwithstanding all this, the two friends made a few salient observations, gathered a few rare examples of the little species of man for their internal bug collection, pinned them up and arranged them in generalized categories.

At 6 P.M. the red automobile, Mercedes 18-24, came by and drove them off to the Krieau.†† There they found an altogether dust-free country air and quiet. A man in a black suit and snow-white gloves mounted a horse. A *fiaker* brought a dancer (the Imperial Opera had just opened), a gray automobile drove up, muffled engine, roaring in a baritone, more than 30 horsepower. The little garden was full of yellow flowers that looked like little sunflowers and the rabbits in their cages pricked up their ears at an irregular slant. The two friends smoked Prinzesas and gaped at the mostly empty white tables and benches. In early spring and fall the place gets really hopping. But it was only August 31!

So the two friends drove on to the winter embankment.

Danube, small track, big leather factory, wobbly granite pave-

---

*The Café-pavilion "Am Graben"
† Horse-drawn hacks
†† A trotting race track in the Prater

ment, good enough for the wide-tired truck rolling along at a snail's pace! But the automobile leapt, galloped, hopped, like a déclassé vehicle on this paved truck road. To the left lay the winter embankment, to the right a raised plateau made of sand and gravel dug out of the Danube studded with young birch trees. From there one had a panoramic view of blue-gray hills, black factory chimneys and the glow of the sunset. In the distance reared the somber dynamite depot, the Laaerberg, the Central Cemetery, the Kahlenberg—. The dark red blaze of the striped sunset surged against the gray molten lead-colored sky and earth. The leather factory reared up like a black beast, and three massive chimneys sent black smoke into the blaze like little spurts of steam that would like to put out giant fires! The slender delicate young birch trees in the Danube landfill trembled in the evening wind and the two friends picked out lovely smooth light brown pebbles as souvenirs of the pleasant evening. Back on the highway waited the red automobile, Mercedes 18-24, which, in fourth gear could rip along like a little roadrunning Orient Express.

The red blaze against the leaden sky turned raspberry colored, then dark gray-red. The two friends remarked: "Now there's nothing more to see. The play is over." So they climbed into the red automobile and said to the chauffeur: "Fourth gear, please—."

They whizzed back to the Grabenkiosk.

Still seated there was the French lady whom one only dared greet with one's eyes.

But at this late hour one felt entitled to say "Good evening—."

And the two gentlemen politely bid her: "Bon soir—."

The Night

The night won't pass. Naturally you keep dwelling all the while on each and every one of your thousand unnecessary sins. Nevertheless or precisely for that very reason, the night won't pass. How foolishly you lived, or rather, failed to live, actually just slid by, dying a little every day. You've got no Bismarck-brain, never took yourself in hand, failed to fulfill man's sole true purpose! A thousand things drove you from yourself, robbed you of your innate, indwelling vitality, drove you away from the best of your self!

That's why the night won't pass.

Because the sum total of your dumb and unnecessary sins is staggering.

Did you really have to that time?! No, you didn't have to at all, especially not in this altogether perilous affair! So why did you go and do it?! So that this neverending night would afford you the human occasion to keep remembering and, as it were, dredging up your stony life of sin, and so that it would keep tormenting you for not having been enough of a man throughout this long preciously petrifying period of your life!

That's why your night won't pass!

Sanatorium for the Mentally Imbalanced (but not the one in which I wiled!)

Morning consultation.

The doctor is seated, like a district attorney, behind a massive desk, with a serious, searching look on his face.

The delinquent (patient) enters.

"Please, have a seat—."

Pause, during which the district attorney (doctor) studies the criminal to ascertain any sign of paralysis or simulation—.

"Now then, my dear Peter Altenberg, seeing as I've known you for quite some time now through your interesting books, I take the liberty of dispensing with the conventional title 'Sir' in the case of a famous person like yourself. Apropos of which, I understand your female admirers address you directly with the initials 'P.A'!? I dare not as of yet permit myself that honorific abbreviation—.

"But let's get down to business! So, my dear Peter Altenberg, what are we going to have for breakfast?!"

"*We*?! That I can't tell you. But I myself take coffee, a light coffee with plenty of milk—."

"Coffee?! Is that so?! Coffee be it then, light coffee with plenty of milk—?!? Coffee, if you please—!"

"Yes, please, it's my regular morning drink, to which I've been accustomed for thirty years now—."

"Very well then. But you are here, in fact, to disabuse yourself of your previous lifestyle, which does not appear to have done you much good, and, more importantly, you are here to acquire the necessary energy to at least attempt to gradually undertake such salubrious changes in your heretofore accustomed, indeed perhaps all too accustomed, lifestyle!?! So, for the moment at least, let's stick with coffee with milk. But why such a pronounced aversion to tea?! One can also sip one's tea diluted with milk—?!"

"Yes, but I prefer to drink coffee with milk—."

"Do you, Mr. Altenberg, have a particular reason for deeming the satisfaction of a morning tea as insufficiently bracing for your nerves?!?"

"Yes, because I don't like the taste of it —."

"Aha, that's just what I wanted to establish. Now then, my dear sir, what do you have with your beloved and seemingly indispensable morning coffee with milk?!?"

"With it?! Nothing!"

"But you must have something solid with it! Coffee on an empty stomach doesn't taste good —."

"No, I have nothing with it; all I like is coffee with milk plain and simple —."

"Well, my dear Sir, with all due respect, that just won't do here. I'm afraid you'll have to concede two rolls with butter —."

"I loathe butter, I loathe rolls, but even more so I loathe buttered rolls!"

"We'll neutralize that aversion in due time! I've brought off far more difficult feats, I assure you, my friend —. So, and now you will be so good as to quietly betake yourself to your breakfast on the veranda. One more thing: Do you customarily rest after breakfast?"

"That depends —."

"That depends won't do. Either you rest or you take a constitutional."

"Alright, so I'll rest —."

"No, you will take a half-hour stroll —!"

The delinquent staggers out of the consultation room and presents himself for a punitive breakfast on the veranda, the punishment sharpened with two buttered rolls.

Several days later. The district attorney: "You see now, my dear famous poet, your facial expression is already much freer, I dare say, more human, not so preoccupied with set ideas —. Did the two buttered rolls do you any harm?! There now!"

No, they did him no harm, since he tore them up daily and scattered the crumbs in the chicken yard —.

Afternoon consultation.

"Mr. Peter Altenberg, to the director's office, on the double —."

"Please be seated.

I strictly forbade the consumption of alcohol —."

"Indeed you did, Mr. Director, Sir —."

"Do you recognize that stack of empty slivovitz bottles?!?"

"Indeed I do, they're mine—."

"They were found today under your bed—."

"Where else should they have been found?! I put them there myself—."

"How did you manage to procure that poison in my asylum?!"

"I bribed someone. Two Crowns were not enough to corrupt his honest conscience. So I offered him three Crowns."

"You're innocent then in this entire matter, but that two-faced orderly is the guilty party! I'll make him answer for this, despite his twenty-five years of service in this institution, in the course of which, as far as I can tell, his conduct was unimpeachable."

"Mr. Director, Sir, just yesterday you remarked to me that, as a consequence of the constancy of my solid lifestyle here in your institution, I looked a good twenty years younger and was hardly recognizable!"

"I made the remark for pedagogical reasons, to fortify your self-confidence—."

"Mr. Director, Sir, may I have the empty slivovitz bottles picked up at your office later?!? I get six Heller a bottle deposit, see—."

Director to the underhanded employee: "Say, Anton, whatever prompted you after twenty-five years of unimpeachable service to allow yourself to be bribed by a patient, even by such a famous quirky poet, and to procure for him such a large quantity of brandy?!?"

"But Mr. Director, Sir, if I hadn't already been doing that for years for hundreds of alcoholics every one of them would've flown the coop after three days and we'd have had an empty asylum!"

"Very well then, Anton, but please make sure from now on that the empty bottles not be found—."

"Mr. Director, Sir, that low-down orderly Franz pulled one on me, he's jealous of all I earn on the side—."

Director to the orderly Franz: "Say, Franz, mind your own business! You make enough already by letting our alcoholics 'have a little go' with our hysterical Misses—. To each his own. In a proper institution like ours order must be maintained!"

Mood

"Today, for Christ's sake, not the slightest little poem or sketch comes to mind, God knows, I'm just not in the mood!" is one of the lies you used to get away with a couple decades ago, say around 1870. Either you haven't slept enough, or jealousy hampers your "mental machinery," a ghastly impediment of all bodily functions, practically prompting "the murderer within," or it's your stomach, your worthy intestine, or "the rent," "the tailor," "the florist," "the waiter," or "ambition," "envy," "humiliation," "injustices," "disappointed expectation," "the promise didn't prove fruitful." Everything, just everything is to blame, or rather for the rest of us, pleasantly impeded your creation of the slightest little poem or sketch! "Mood" is one of those common lies! The "unhampered" organism is always in the mood! You ought to see me when somebody in parting presses twenty Crowns into my hand! It happened once years ago, and the magazine to which I was at that time an active contributor, previously inactive, wrote me: "Please do put a lid on your perfidious productivity." (Der 'März,' Munich, Kurt Aram, Editor!) "Mood" is nonsense, a lie, a swindle. It's enough to spawn perplexed amazement in "psychopaths!" Not to be in a "mood?!" That's impossible. There are only "somatic" causes, all matters of the mind, of the spirit are merely a necessary consequence of the overall machinery. Loosen the little screws, and the valves, and the "mood" must out! When the machinery's in working order, the mind and spirit work to capacity! Often beyond capacity.

July Sunday

Five in the morning. All is bathed in yellow sunlight. The air is still fresh and cool. Many tourists tear themselves out of sleep, suffer sleep deprivation, just to greet the sun. It'll be easy for them to banish their sleepiness with a splash of cold water. It's still cool out and you march into the hot day as into the heat of battle!

Far too few offer up their utmost to meet the day and the hour. And even the most contented heart longs for the extraordinary. Here comes the July Sunday in glaring yellow light! July Sunday, be the bearer of what we long for!

Everywhere you look, unhappy humanity is escaping. Running, exhausted, we fall in line, back to the daily grind! Monday, how sour you would be were you not the source and reason for Sunday's sweet anticipated pleasure! On Sundays, you see the weary plunked down in meadows and woods, washed clean of last week's filth, prepared to tackle the coming week.

In the Stadtpark

As children we sat with our beloved parents evening after evening in the Stadtpark on the terrace of the Kursalon. We were served ice cream and cookie twirls and didn't have a care in the world. For years now, father has not set foot outside his cozy room, nor mother her cozy sepulcher. Bald and careworn, I wend my way through the Stadtpark, to the terrace of the Kursalon, where I select the very same table at which we once sat so carefree with our beloved parents. I order the same flavor ice cream as I did back then, raspberry-chocolate, with plenty of crispy fresh cookie twirls. The flower bed is just as it was, perhaps a little more colorful, the arrangement a mite more original. I see parents with their children. They argue and scold. Our parents never argued and scolded — never. Maybe it was bad that they didn't, but they had respect for their own little creations, and confidence in us too! We disappointed them; but they accepted this as their lot and our destiny. We never noticed the tears they shed over us — . Now I sit, bald-headed, careworn, in the Stadtpark, on the terrace of the Kursalon, at the very same table where we once sat without our beloved parents, eat the same dish of raspberry-chocolate ice cream as before, with plenty of crispy fresh cookie twirls — . The flower bed I look down on is a little more colorful, the arrangement a mite more original. But otherwise, nothing has changed from those days of dumb childhood to these nights of tired age! I see parents scolding their children in the park; our parents never scolded us; they hoped that we would one day repay their kindness, but we never did. We had a lovely childhood; and so we sink into memory, since the present has hardly enough substance to live on. Our parents were all too gentle, hopeful, too ready to bow to destiny. It was a curse and a blessing! For now we can look back on days that were idyllic — . Not everyone who sees the darkness closing in can look back with a thankful and loving heart on the lightness of former days — .

A Sunday (12.29.1918)*

So then they all sat around him in the dear little café with the brown-yellow wallpaper and everyone, every last one of them, wanted to help, but naturally nobody had even the slightest inkling of the constant inconceivable havoc he had to endure in that ravaged brain and spinal cord (like the husk of a living corpse), his nervous system laid low by excessive use of sleeping pills (Paraldehyd), while all other organs remained, despite his 60 years, in impeccable working order. They drank tea with raspberry syrup, chocolate, coffee, they ate bread with butter, and one of them even had ham with his buttered bread. No one suspected what destruction, wrack and ruin the poet suffered, but everyone naturally tried in the most inept way to be of some assistance to this curious creature who meant so much to his friends, treasured by each on account of his own special purpose and aspirations, dreams and despair, indeed for the sum total of his own oh-so-complicated existence inscrutable to himself; everyone tried to help save the poet from sliding into the abyss, and simultaneously, to help save himself! To no avail.

He had sunk deep into the swamp of the sinful abuse of his sleeping pills, and the concern of his few true friends just slid off him like little globs of quicksilver sliding off a glass plate!

They all sat around him in the dear little café with the brown-yellow wallpaper, sipping tea with raspberry syrup, chocolate (1918!), shots of Schwechater, double malt beer etc., etc., etc., wanted to help, help, help, and yet had not the faintest notion of just how the poet was being ripped apart from inside out, a living corpse, his very essence expunged. No help is possible, no friendship, no selfless surrender, when the stubborn brain, consumed by its own sickness, almost deliberately, it seems, forsakes what could still be saved. So one by one, at irregular intervals, the friends all take their leave, deeply disappointed, and you are obliged to endure your last torments, to live through them alone! You won't

_____

* Published posthumously

· 136

drag anyone along on life's, nay, death's slide into the abyss; every him, every her cuts and runs from you, the anointed one, in that last fearful hour; they can't do anything more for you than they've already done! Farewell, luckless poet who gave us all the gift of his soul and did himself in with it!

Farewell!

To Make a Long Story Short:
The Prose of Peter Altenberg (an afterword)

His walrus mustache was emblematic, like Walt Whitman's wild wooly beard: no mere untrimmed tuft growing wild, but a Zeitgeist gage, a canny alley cat's whiskers tailor-made to fit through tight fixes. And like the bewhiskered Brooklyn bard, to whom he has been compared—in stance, not style—Peter Altenberg (1859–1919), the turn-of-the-century Viennese raconteur-scribe, was a walker and a talker and an inveterate loll-about. Both had a penchant for lyrical digression and irregular punctuation, but the similarity stops there. For while Whitman went on at length in epic outbursts of freewheeling verse, Altenberg choked back the flow.

His own avowed paradigm for the pearls he spit out, most while propped up in bed in bouts of chronic insomnia, was Charles Baudelaire's *Spleen de Paris* (1869). Yet whereas Baudelaire's pioneering work comprises texts that tease and test but never forsake the playing field of poetry, Altenberg extracted the poetic essence of impressions and spat them out in spare narratives situated to the prose side of the divide.

Other formal influences include the "Correspondenzkarte," the world's first postcard launched and disseminated in Austria in 1869, which subsequently sparked a vogue; and the Feuilleton, a lyrical form of first person journalistic prose often of a decidedly purple slant produced by, among other Viennese wordsmiths of the day, the young Theodor Herzl before the latter forsook belles lettres for the nation-building business.

The artfully crafted fairy tales of the great Dane, Hans Christian Andersen, have been noted as yet another influence. And Altenberg's writings can indeed be read as pruned Märchen minus the "once upon a time" and without any pretense of a "happily ever after." "We relegated fairy tales to the realm of childhood, that exceptional, wondrous, stirring, remarkable time of life!" he wrote (in a text entitled *Retrospective Introduction to My Book, Märchen des Lebens* [The Fairy Tale of Life], 1908).

But why rig out childhood with it, when childhood is already suffi-
ciently romantic and fairytale-like in and of itself?!? The disen-
chanted adult had best seek out the fairytale-like elements, the
romanticism of each day and each hour right here and now in the
hard, stern, cold fundament of life!

Disenchanted adult or overgrown child, Altenberg never quite
managed to break out of his self-constructed cocoon, except on
the butterfly wings of his writing and the charmed cadences of his
café conversation. Like his English contemporary, Lewis Carroll
(1832–1898), Altenberg idealized childhood as the indigenous
province of poetry and adulated children as its natural priests and
purveyors. Like Carroll, he also flirted with a photographic
(though to my knowledge, never practiced) pedophilia, prizing
above all his possessions a collection of suggestive postcards,
many of pre-pubescent girls. Like Carroll, he too managed to
metamorphose (or sublimate) his worship of young girls into the
stuff of literature. Did not Dante do the same with his Beatrice fix-
ation and Petrarch with his predilection for Laura?

The fact that Altenberg clung psychologically to the province of
childhood, reticent to forsake its cozy confines for the constant
compromise and abject spiritual poverty of adulthood, can either
be viewed—depending on your point of view—as indisputable
proof of imaginative fortitude or a telltale sign of the emotional
frailty that landed him in a mental asylum and ultimately led to his
psychological and physical collapse. His Viennese contemporary,
Sigmund Freud, would have had a field day analyzing a rife knot of
neuroses, but analysis was not Altenberg's inclination or forte and
his neuroses proved nourishing. Thirteen books and a copious
posthumous opus, including reams of letters and inscribed postcards, attest to a prodigious and prescient verbal fortitude that
outlived his own collapse and that of the world that produced him.

Born into a prosperous assimilated Jewish family in Vienna in
1859, the young Richard Engländer (who later took the pen name
Peter Altenberg) was labeled by a grade school teacher as a "genius
without abilities." The characterization bears a striking parallel to

the title of the great Viennese novel, *The Man Without Qualities*, by Robert Musil (an ardent Altenberg fan), the first part of which appeared in print in 1931. Altenberg described himself as "the man without compromises," in a concise five-and-a-quarter page long "Autobiography," in his third book, *Was der Tag mir zuträgt* [What the Day Brings], 1901.

He flunked the writing segment of his high school graduation exam, as self-promulgated apocryphal legend has it, responding tersely to the theme: "The Influence of the New World," with a single word: "potatoes." Passing the test a year later, he took up and promptly abandoned the study of medicine, botany and the law, respectively, and half-heartedly explored the business of selling books, before finally concluding that he preferred to write them.

In 1883, a psychiatrist hired by his concerned father diagnosed "over-excitation of the nervous system" and concluded an "incapacity for employment." Altenberg took it as a one-way ticket to Literary Bohemia and the life of the coffeehouse poet, of which he became the epitome, and never looked back. His befuddled, albeit tolerant, father provided a modest living allowance until the family business (subsequently bequeathed to a brother) went bust, leaving the down at the heels Bohemian henceforth beholden to the fickle kindness of strangers. The grateful son wrote of his father in the aforementioned "Autobiography":

He [the father] was once asked: "Aren't you proud of your son?!"
He replied: "I was not overly vexed that he remained an idler for 30 years. So I'm not overly honored that he's a poet now! I gave him his freedom. I knew that it was a long shot. I counted on his soul."

Long before his words found their way into newspapers and periodicals, Altenberg was well-known as a vetted Viennese eccentric who lodged in various hotels and traipsed around town in baggy clothes of his own conception (he was a pioneer in leisure wear), curious walking sticks and open sandals whatever the weather, favoring the companionship of young girls and loose women. He gave out as his official address the Café Central—also the sometime haunt of Russian émigrés Leon Trotsky and his chess partner Vladimir Ilyich Lenin—where Altenberg presided over his own table of garrulous caffeine-primed regulars.

How and when he first broke into print is the stuff of another homespun legend. One day, the author recalls, the members of Vienna's ascendant literary avant-garde, Jung Wien, caught him scribbling away at his café table and immediately recognized his talent. The poet Richard Beer-Hoffmann is said to have first appreciated his writing, but it was the brilliantly sardonic critic Karl Kraus who sent Altenberg's fledgling selection of prose to S. Fischer Verlag, the foremost German publisher of the day, which promptly published his first book, *Wie Ich Es Sehe* [How I See It] in 1896. The book was a popular sensation and immediately put its author on the map.

"If it be permitted to speak of 'love at first sound,' then that's what I experienced in my first encounter with this poet of prose," wrote Thomas Mann. Other impassioned literary partisans included the playwright Arthur Schnitzler, the poet and librettist Hugo von Hofmannstahl, and Felix Salten, the versatile author of, among other works, the children's book classic *Bambi* and the underground pornographic classic *The Adventures of Josephine Munzenbacher*.

Salten's incisive description of Altenberg's prose bears mention:

Some [of his pieces] are like steel projectiles, so tightly enclosed in themselves, so complete and precise in their form; and like projectiles, they pierce the breast; you are struck and you bleed. Some are like crystals and diamonds, sparkling in the multicolored reflections of the light of life, gleaming with captured rays of sunlight and glittering with a hidden inner fire. Some are like ripe fruits, warm with the waft of summer, swollen and sweet . . .

And just next door in Prague, the young Franz Kafka took Altenberg's terse writing style to heart and mind as a literary model for his own work. "In his small stories," Kafka observed,

his whole life is mirrored. And every step, every movement he makes confirms the truth of his words. Peter Altenberg is a genius of nullifications, a singular idealist who discovers the splendors of this world like cigarette butts in the ashtrays of coffeehouses.

Coffeehouse poet par excellence, Altenberg claimed to toss off his texts in a cavalier fashion for the throw-away pages of weekly and daily newspapers. "I view writing as a natural organic spilling out of a full, overripe person," he wrote in a letter to Schnitzler. "I hate any revision. Toss it off and that's good — ! Or bad! What's the difference?!"

But tossed off, carefully crafted or both, there is nothing sloppy about his spare aesthetic. The extreme economy of his sketches sometimes reads more Japanese than Viennese — an elective affinity born out by the caption he inscribed for a lady friend on a postcard of Japanese women posing under blossoming cherry trees:

The Japanese paint a blossoming branch — and it is spring in its entirety! We paint all of spring — and it's hardly a blossoming branch!

His Japanophile propensity is reiterated in the sketch "In Munich," in which he presses his stuffy fellow Europeans to "Learn from the Japanese!" lauding the latter as "an artistic people."

Altenberg's first direct exposure to the Japanese sensibility occurred at the Sixth Exhibition of the Wiener Secession in 1900, a show exclusively devoted to the art of Japan though chronologically too late to have influenced his style, which appears to have sprouted Athena-like out of his brain and remained more or less unchanged throughout the two decades of his active writing career, this encounter with an alien world view must have felt strangely affirmative, more homecoming than departure, more mirror than window.

It was not his first flirtation with the exotic. Altenberg's second book, *Ashantee*, published in 1897, recounts his dealings with and vivid impressions of the inhabitants of an African show-village on display for a year as a live exhibit in Vienna's zoological garden. The grotesquery of the very premise of such an exhibition is lampooned in a short reflection entitled "Philosophy":

Visitors to the Ashanti Village knock in the evening on the wooden walls of the huts for a lark.

> *The goldsmith Nôthëi: "Sir, if you came to us in Accra as objects on exhibit, we wouldn't knock on the walls of your huts in the evening!"*

Yet rather than stand above it all and wag a virtuous finger at the crude voyeurism of Viennese visitors, for whom the Africans on display were little more than talking animals, Altenberg deconstructs the spectacle by stepping inside it. He falls in love and loses his heart to various black girls and ladies "on display" and peals off their shell of otherness—an otherness he knew all too well under his own white skin, as a baptized Jew trying to pass in an often hostile world given to Catholic piety and Teutonic cult.

But while Altenberg the author let his imagination wander to exotic climes and loved to wax eloquent about Nature, à la Ralph Waldo Emerson, Altenberg the man was a hopeless homebody, a die-hard city slicker who dared not venture outside his beloved Vienna, except to revisit nearby Austrian spas and resorts cherished in childhood, and on a few occasions, to soak up the sun and surf on the Lido outside Venice. A piece entitled "Traveling" is, in fact, devoted to the "dirt-cheap pleasure altogether free of disappointments, to study the train schedule from mid-May on and pick out the very train with which you would, if only . . ."—in short, the pleasure of staying put.

Perils lurked outside the safe periphery of the urban grid. Altenberg's Nature is at once an idealized locale and a metaphor for an unleashed sexuality which he both craved and feared. Consider the unabashed phallic fantasy that underlies the following paean to the great outdoors from the aforementioned "Autobiography":

> *As a boy I had an indescribable love for mountain meadows. The mountain meadow steaming under the blazing sun, fragrantly wafting, alive with bugs and butterflies, made me downright drunk. So too did clearings in the woods. On swampy sunny patches sit butterflies, blue silken small ones and black and red admirals and you can see the hoof print of deer. But for mountain meadows I had a fanatical love, I longed for them. Under all the white hot stones I imagined there lurked poison adders, and this creature was the very*

incarnation of the fairy tale mystery of my boyhood years. It replaced the man-eating ogre, the giant and the witch. All the bites and their consequences, the terribly slow and torturous pain, I knew it all by heart, how to treat a wound and so on. The wondrously delicate gray-black body of the adder seemed to me to be the loveliest, most elegant creature, and when I loved a little girl I always pictured again and again only one thing happening: an adder bit her in the foot on a hike and I sucked out the venom to save her!

Enamored as he was of Nature's lure, he preferred to take it in limited doses. In the same text, he admits to never actually having seen an adder. "It remained for me a bad but sweetly disturbing dream."

Readers disinclined to the short form may indeed find Altenberg's sketches a bit claustrophobic and his attachment to his native stomping ground positively suffocating. It may seem at times as if he managed to stretch the city itself into a giant nursery navigated on a hopscotch grid. And though Altenberg's Vienna is peopled with pimps and prostitutes, cabbies and call girls, florists and floozies, there is a certain childlike innocence about them all. The hookers may not all wear their hearts on their sleeve, but they won't give you the clap. And some of them, like the hired subject of "Poem," even write verse. His cast of characters comprise a collection of more or less accommodating playmates in an elaborate game with rules of his own devising. Even the most venomous types have been defanged. In "My Gmunden," a mysterious stranger with paranoid delusions encountered, notably not in Vienna but in the resort town of Gmunden, pulls out a Browning revolver and bids the narrator enjoy his supper—"Because it's your last!" In the story, the threatening stranger becomes an odd sort of Doppelgänger, a troubled comrade in arms, a fellow *Meshuganeh*.

In the short form, Altenberg isolated and delineated pleasures and pitfalls, savoring the former and attenuating the sting of the latter, compressing life into tiny parcels of manageable experience and prescribing them like pills to his reader.

He played his own heartstrings like a harp, plucking and letting go, teasing himself into a neverending state of excitation, and in the process eliciting a flurry of charged preludes. Whether taken as crystallized spasms of a crippled libido or as grains of irritation compounded into pearls, these texts transcend the moment of their creation and cry out with a remarkable modernity.

While such celebrated Fin-de-Siècle literati as Arthur Schnitzler and Hugo von Hofmannstahl read dated and a bit dowdy today, the sputtering sparks of a fire gone cold, Altenberg's clipped "telegram style" resonates like bolts of prescient lightning leaping from one turn of the century to the next. "Only in the era of telegraphy, lightning fast trains and automobile-cabs," wrote his friend and promoter, Egon Friedell, "could there emerge such a poet whose passionate desire it is to always stick to the essential."

Western Union has since given way to AOL and the trains and cars have accelerated considerably. The angst-ridden rapid-fire era of the telegram and the tommy-gun has spawned the frenetic age of email and e-war, with love and death on demand at the press of a button. Raised on the knowledge that an atom of matter is all it takes to make a pretty big bang, we've refined our taste for the essential. $E=MC^2$, the concise epic of the 20th century, is, after all, only three letters long. Now that we've turned the corner into the 21st century, Altenberg's telegrams of the soul read right up to date.

Peter Wortsman

P.S. (to P.A. from P.W.)

P.A. gripped the frames of his spectacles, wavering between the urge to crush them and to slip them into his inside pocket. Portable windows, he called them and laughingly imagined replacing the lenses with stained shards stolen from the Sainte Chapelle in Paris. It would lend me, he would tell his friends, a more colorful imagination. He took out a pen to jot down the thought, but the weight of the gold-tipped fountain pen (a gift from a female admirer) was suddenly more than he could bear, and besides, he had no paper. Waiter, he called, bring me another slivovitz. It was his fifth of the afternoon. Another could not hurt and perhaps it would loosen the tightness he felt in his brain. In a dream the night before, he had witnessed the digging of the Erie Canal, watched nubile young girls obliged to ride naked and bareback on Indian elephants drawing barges behind. He awakened to the frightening spectacle of their revolt, girls and elephants charging at him out of his sweat-soaked pillow. Waiter, he called, bring me a sheet of paper. I want to note down how curious it is to feel the flesh of non-existent women. The waiter shook his head and smiled, accustomed to the habits of the poet.

P.W.

Telegrams of the Soul was designed by David Bullen Design
and printed at The Stinehour Press in Lunenburg, Vermont.
The paper is 60lb Mohawk Vellum.

DATE DUE

GAYLORD No. 2333   PRINTED IN U.S.A.